HOME away from HOME

CYNTHIA LORD

HOME away from HOME

Scholastic Press / New York

Library of Congress Cataloging-in-Publication Data

Names: Lord, Cynthia, author.

Title: Home away from home / Cynthia Lord.

Description: First edition. | New York : Scholastic Inc., 2023. | Audience:
Ages 8–12. | Audience: Grades 7–9. | Summary: Mia is spending her summer
with her grandmother in a small Maine town, expecting it to be an oasis of stability in her
changing life, but there is a new know-it-all boy next door, and soon she finds herself competing
with Cayman in identifying an injured bird of prey—and pretty much everything else.

Identifiers: LCCN 2022034018 (print) | LCCN 2022034019 (ebook) |
ISBN 9781338726114 (hardcover) | ISBN 9781338726121 (ebook)

Subjects: LCSH: Grandmothers—Juvenile fiction. | Wildlife rescue—Juvenile fiction. |
Gyrfalcon—Juvenile fiction. | Neighbors—Juvenile fiction. | Friendship—Juvenile fiction. |
Maine—Juvenile fiction. | CYAC: Grandmothers—Fiction. | Wildlife rescue—Fiction. |
Neighbors—Fiction. | Friendship—Fiction. | Gyrfalcon—Fiction. | Maine—Fiction. |
BISAC: JUVENILE FICTION / Social Themes / Friendship | JUVENILE FICTION /
Social Themes / New Experience

Classification: LCC PZ7.L87734 Hom 2023 (print) | LCC PZ7.L87734 (ebook) |
DDC 813.6 [Fic]—dc23/eng/20220808

LC record available at https://lccn.loc.gov/2022034018

LC ebook record available at https://lccn.loc.gov/2022034019

10 9 8 7 6 5 4 3 2 1   23 24 25 26 27

Printed in Italy   183

First edition, April 2023

Book design by Elizabeth B. Parisi

To Kate

Chapter 1

"GPS says the road is coming up," I announced from the back seat of the rental car. We'd been traveling for hours, and I could barely sit still now that we were close. "I remember there's a Dunkin' right before you turn."

"It's okay, Mia," Mom said. "Scott knows the way. Just put down your phone and enjoy the view."

If I hadn't said anything, I was pretty sure Scott would've missed the road, though. Mom and I had come to Grandma's every summer since I was born. But Scott had only been Mom's boyfriend for a year, and he'd only been to Grandma's once with us before.

Stone Harbor, Maine, was at the end of a long peninsula, a crooked finger of land pointing out into the ocean. There was only one road to get to there, so no one ever just passed through—you had to mean to come. Grandma always said she liked it that way. It kept the town small and the neighbors close.

"Too close," Mom always replied.

But I loved how nothing big ever changed there.

I couldn't wait to do all my usual Maine summer things: put my feet in the (freezing!) ocean, walk to Holbrook's store, look for seals in the harbor and eagles at the Point, do jigsaw puzzles and play games with Grandma—things that might seem small at home but were fun here.

This year I had an extra reason to come, though. Mom and I were moving, and it hurt too much to be home.

"Mom, make sure you don't give away any of my books," I said, leaning forward between the front seats. "I didn't have time to look through them all."

"I'll text you a photo of your bookcase when I get home," Mom said. "You can let me know which ones you want to keep."

"Okay," I said, leaning back again. I hoped she'd remember.

When Mom had said she and Scott were moving in together, I had been okay with it because I thought Scott would move in with *us*. I liked Scott well enough. He was always nice to me, even though I don't think he ever really wanted a kid. He liked plans and for everything to be organized and neat.

But then Mom had said they were buying a new house together and selling ours.

"It'll be a new start," she'd said.

A new start meant leaving something old behind, though. I thought Mom felt like I did. Like our house was a part of us, practically a family member. Not somewhere you just *leave*. Dad had moved right after the divorce, but I never thought Mom and I would.

Ken the Realtor had given Mom a long list of changes to get our house ready to sell. He'd gone room to room, pointing out anything that was too old or too "us," like family photos. "Buyers want to imagine their own things in each room," he'd said. "So the house will show better if you put those away."

When Ken had gotten to my room, he'd said it looked too much like a kid's room. He'd suggested we take down my artwork and posters, repaint my turquoise walls gray, and put most of my clothes, sports gear, and books into storage. "Buyers might want this room to be an office," he had said. "We want them to see the possibilities!"

I did try. I took down my posters and artwork. I emptied my closet and packed my sports gear into boxes.

But when Mom had opened the can of gray paint, I cried. The color looked like nothing.

"This is only so we can sell it," Mom said gently. "In the new house, you can paint your room any color you want."

I had nodded, but this room had been mine for my whole life. Painting it for strangers felt wrong, like a big gray eraser wiping me away.

That night Mom had called Grandma and asked if I could come to Maine by myself that year while she and Scott made the rest of Ken the Realtor's changes.

As Scott turned the car onto the road to Stone Harbor, I felt my worries unwind a little. Now every salt marsh and field felt familiar, like I belonged here and was coming home again. Grandma called her house my "home away from home," even though Maine was a plane ride away from our house in Ohio.

We passed the field where the goats always joined us for a walk along their side of the fence. And the place where Grandma once coaxed a huge snapping turtle across the road so he didn't get squished.

"Here's where Dad taught me to ride my bike!" I said as we passed the cemetery. "Remember, Mom? I rode up and down the pathways, but then I scratched my leg on a gravestone." I laughed. "Dad carried me, and you rode my little bike back to Grandma's."

"I do remember," she said.

"Mia learned to ride a bike *in a cemetery?*" Scott asked Mom.

She shrugged. "There isn't a park here. We thought the cemetery was safer than riding in the road. Looking back, it was a bad idea."

My smile faded. "It was just a scratch," I mumbled.

I liked remembering that day. Riding around the gravestones, Dad carrying me, Mom riding my bike. I thought she'd laugh, too. But that was the last year Dad came to Maine with us. He and Mom had an argument and he left early. I didn't like remembering that, but most happy memories of that summer led to hard ones eventually.

Mom turned to look at me in the back seat. "I wish we could stay, Mia," she said. "Are you sure you'll be okay here by yourself? A month is a long time."

"Of course I'll be okay. I'm eleven!" I said, rolling my

eyes. "And I won't be by myself. I'll be with Grandma."

Mom sighed. "That's what I'm worried about. Keep her out of trouble, all right?"

I grinned. "I'll try."

Being at Grandma's was different from being at home. Grandma let me do things that Mom didn't. I could read books in bed way past bedtime, eat junk food, and walk around town by myself.

Grandma didn't like to plan ahead, so I didn't have a schedule at her house. Grandma just got up in the morning, looked outside at the weather, and decided what to do. One day she'd said it was a good day to look for moose. So we drove hours to find one. Mom had said we were lost, but Grandma said, "We'll figure it out as we go."

And we did.

As Scott turned the corner, I leaned forward again. "That's Grandma's mailbox!" I said. "The white one with the dog bowl on the ground."

Grandma didn't even have a dog. She put that bowl of water out for people walking their dogs. Grandma was the only adult I knew who loved animals as much as I did.

Her house looked like many old farmhouses, white with a bay window and a porch with rocking chairs. But instead of painting the doors, shutters, and rocking chairs gray or green, Grandma painted hers bright lemon yellow.

Waving to us from the porch, Grandma looked like she always did in the summer: knee-length shorts streaked with garden dirt, a floppy T-shirt, sandals, and a wide-brimmed straw hat.

Scott pulled into the driveway, and I grabbed my suitcase off the seat beside me before he even stopped the car.

"Welcome home away from home!" Grandma said as I ran up the steps. She wrapped me in a giant hug. "You're finally here!"

"We aren't late, are we?" I heard Scott ask Mom behind me. "The plane was on time, and we didn't stop anywhere."

But I knew what Grandma meant, because I felt the same way.

I was finally here.

Mom gave Grandma a big hug, too. "There's another suitcase in the trunk," she said. "I think Mia brought enough stuff to stay all summer!"

"I wish!" Grandma said. Then while Mom helped Scott get the rest of my luggage, she leaned in so only I could hear. "Look for a secret in your top dresser drawer."

I grinned. "I'll be right back!"

Inside the house, the familiar smell of old wood and damp salt air comforted me. Looking around the kitchen, I was relieved that nothing big had changed.

I didn't need to ask where to find the scissors or which drawer to open for a spoon or which cupboard held juice glasses. I already knew, just as I knew Grandma would have vanilla ice cream in the freezer. Vanilla was my favorite when I was in kindergarten, and I'd never told Grandma that I liked chocolate chip better now. While I was in Maine, vanilla was still my favorite.

I peeked inside each room I passed. The living room couch reminded me of books Grandma and I'd read together there. The downstairs bathroom was where I had once hid a bucket of sea snails to bring home as pets— until Mom and Dad found them and made me put them back in the ocean. Grandma's bedroom filled me with a cozy, safe feeling, because she let me sleep with her during thunderstorms.

Upstairs, my room was just as I remembered—except for the jar of purple irises on the nightstand and the stack of clean towels on my bed.

Through the window, I could hear gulls calling and

see all the way over barn weathervanes and house rooftops to the harbor.

I set down my suitcase and opened the top dresser drawer. Inside was a family-sized package of M&M'S.

Grandma knew Mom wouldn't approve, so it was our secret. I pulled out my phone and took a photo of the candy to remember it forever. Then I took photos of my room.

I wished I'd thought to do that back in Ohio before we made changes to my room and started packing. It was too late now, though. It all looked different.

As I came back down the stairs, I heard Mom in the kitchen.

"I suppose we have time for a short walk," she said to Grandma. "I would like to see downtown before we leave."

"That'll take about two minutes," I joked. Stone Harbor didn't have much of a downtown.

Grandma looked over at me and winked. "Did you find everything in your room?"

I winked back. "Yes, thank you. It was very *sweet* of you."

Following them down the front steps, I felt lighter. The

sun was warm on my hair, and the salt air tasted sharper than the air at home.

Everything was just the way I hoped it would be at Grandma's. Cozy and familiar, with only fun little surprises, like finding treats in my top dresser drawer.

Not big, hard surprises, like finding out things had changed without me. I'd had enough of those surprises to last me a lifetime.

But one problem with surprises is that they're sneaky.

You never know what kind is coming next.

Chapter 2

Walking down the hill toward the harbor, I pulled in a deep breath of salt air. Stone Harbor's downtown was only two rows of white or gray shingled buildings, facing one another across the road. Holbrook's General Store was at one end and the Stone Harbor Community Church was at the other. In between those was a library, a post office, an antiques store, a restaurant, two gift shops, a hardware store, and a real-estate agency with photos of houses for sale in the front window. Beyond the buildings was the ocean, sparkling in the sun, fancy sailboats and squat fishing boats bobbing on the waves.

At home in Ohio, our downtown went on for blocks with boxy brick buildings, fat sidewalks, and lampposts with hanging baskets. There were clothing shops, bookstores, and so many different kinds of restaurants that you could eat a different kind of food every day for weeks. My favorite restaurants were Thai and Indian. Mom would park at one of the parking meters, call in a takeout order, and we'd go store to store to get everything we needed before picking up dinner.

But here in Stone Harbor, if Holbrook's didn't have what you needed, you had to drive at least half an hour to get it. Or order it online. Or borrow it from someone else.

And takeout was mostly ice cream, seafood, and burgers.

Up ahead, Mr. Holbrook was outside filling the store's newspaper rack. He looked older than I remembered. His hair was almost all white now.

"Look who flew in from Ohio!" Grandma yelled to him.

When I was little, I thought it was funny when Grandma said that, like Mom and I got here by flapping our arms like gulls. Now I couldn't help feeling a little embarrassed that Grandma was yelling across the street for everyone to hear.

"How do, Beanie!" Mr. Holbrook adjusted his glasses. "My goodness, is that Mia?"

Mom blushed. No one says "how do" or calls her Beanie in Ohio. She was Beatrix or Dr. Fortin there, a scientist. But here, where she grew up, she was always Beanie. She was remembered as the captain of the girls' high school basketball team the year they won the state championship. And the girl who waitressed every summer at the restaurant to put herself through college.

"Good to see you, Mr. Holbrook," Mom said. "We're here to drop Mia off for a visit."

"Mia and I have so many things to do that I may never send her home!" Grandma said.

Scott looked around. "So many things to do?"

"Oh yes. We have a very long to-do list!" Grandma said. "There are fireflies to watch for. We must hunt for crabs in the tidepools. We have books to borrow from the library. The strawberries need picking, and the church is having a rummage sale soon. Oh, and I saw a new mini golf place near Boothbay! We must try it out. But first we need ice cream!"

I grinned. A to-do list at home meant chores.

Scott looked at Mom. "But we haven't had lunch yet."

Mom took a deep breath, like she was swallowing words she wanted to say.

I ignored them, because at Grandma's house, she's the boss. "And don't forget that we need to take a picnic to the Point," I said, catching up to her. "I want to see the eagles. Did Rachel and HW have babies this year?"

A few years ago, the Stone Harbor Library held a fundraiser, and the high bidder got to name the bald eagle pair that nested at the Point. The winner chose Henry Wadsworth Longfellow and Rachel Carson to honor two writers who loved Maine. Now they're called HW and Rachel for short.

There were eagles in Ohio, too, but not where I lived. They liked wild places and mostly nested near big lakes and marshes and along rivers. At home I certainly couldn't walk to see them, like here.

Mr. Holbrook held the door open for us. "Yes, they had two eaglets this year! You can see the eaglets' heads above the edge of the nest now," he said. "Thank goodness the lady who bought the old Harding place last winter still lets people use the path to go see them. It cuts across her property, so it's nice of her to allow it."

Allow it? It never occurred to me that path belonged to someone. It just seemed like everyone's.

The path was like something in a fairy tale, with soft green moss covering the rocks, little woodland flowers and mushrooms just off the trail, and all around, so many tall dark trees. At the end of the trail, there was a bend around a huge rock and then, just like magic, everything changed. Suddenly, the ocean was ahead. I always had to pause and blink to adjust my eyes from the dark woods to the sun on the rocks and waves.

I couldn't wait to walk down that path again.

Mr. Holbrook stepped behind the store's glass-topped freezer. "What flavor can I get ya?"

I looked at each open bucket of colorful ice cream, even though I already knew my choice. "Small vanilla in a sugar cone."

"You got it!" Mr. Holbrook turned to Grandma. "Peppermint twist?"

She nodded. "Of course!"

Scott and Mom said no ice cream for them. "We're planning to stop for lunch on the way back to Portland," Scott explained. "In fact, we should head out soon. Just in case there's traffic."

I could've told him that there wasn't *ever* much traffic, but I didn't. Scott seemed anxious to get away, and I wanted my alone time with Grandma to start.

Grandma was the only person I didn't have to share with anyone else. I had to share Mom with Scott. I shared Dad with his new wife and baby. And though I loved them all, sometimes I missed being the center of Mom and Dad's world. Now I felt like I half belonged in two places, instead of truly belonging in one.

But as soon as Mom left, Grandma would be all mine. I wanted to tell her the mixed feelings I had about moving. Things I'd been holding inside, not wanting to spoil Mom's excitement for our new start. Or give Dad a reason to complain about Mom.

But those feelings had bottled up to the point of overflowing.

"Always great to see you, Beanie," Mr. Holbrook said. "We miss your sweet smile around here—and your three-point shot! The girls' basketball team barely broke even this year."

Mom smiled. "It's great to see you, too, Mr. H."

She put her arm around me on the walk back to

Grandma's. "I'm glad you'll be here having fun, Sweet Pea. But I'll be thinking of you every day."

"I'll be thinking of you, too, *Beanie*," I teased, licking a vanilla drip off my finger.

She rolled her eyes. "I don't think Mr. H will ever see me as a grown-up."

At the car, I held on to Mom tightly. I'd been looking forward to being here by myself, but now that she was leaving, I was surprised to feel a bit lonely. "I'm sorry you'll have to do all the packing by yourself," I said. "I wanted to help, but it's really hard."

"I know," Mom said, giving me a squeeze. "It's harder than I thought it would be, too."

"Really?" I asked.

"Of course!" she said. "That house has been our home for a long time. I can't help feeling a little sad to leave it. There are a lot of memories there."

I felt closer to Mom, knowing she felt that way, too— even if it was just a little bit. "I love you," I said, not letting go, even though I could feel more ice cream melting down my wrist.

"Love you more," she said. "And I will miss you terribly. But I know you'll have a great time with Grandma.

Scott and I will take care of everything at home."

I nodded. "Thanks. I'll send you lots of photos."

"I'd like some," she said. "But please don't be on your phone all the time, okay? I'm trusting you to remember our phone rules." She turned to Grandma. "At home she has a two-hour screen time limit."

"I'll keep Mia very busy," Grandma promised.

"Don't worry. I'll be having too much fun to overdo it," I promised, licking the ice cream off my arm. "And I told all my friends that I'm on vacation."

Mom gave me a last squeeze. "Do you want me to keep you updated on the move? Or would you like to forget about it?"

I thought for a minute. "I think I'd like to forget about it. Is that okay?"

"Of course," Mom said.

"See you in a few weeks!" Scott said.

As they got into the car, I called to them, "Don't throw away anything that's mine!"

"I won't!" Mom called back.

"Good luck with packing and painting!" I added, anxious to cram everything I had to say into seconds. "I hope—"

But I couldn't bring myself to say, "I hope you sell the house." Because I didn't.

"You have a good flight," I said instead.

Grandma and I finished our ice cream on the front porch. We waved while Scott backed the car out of the driveway and kept waving until the car was out of sight. The next time I saw them, would they have a new house?

"What would you like to do first?" Grandma asked.

I swallowed hard. On the way, I thought I'd immediately jump into being here when Mom and Scott left. I'd forget all about Ohio and enjoy being in Maine, like flipping a switch off and on. But instead I felt like my heart wasn't really here yet. And I'd forgotten something important back in Ohio.

"I don't know," I said. "You choose." Grandma could always be counted on to come up with a fun idea. And I didn't really care what we did as long as we did it together.

"Come see the garden, then. The flowers have missed you," Grandma said. "And I'll introduce you to Miss Agatha."

"Who?" I asked.

Knowing Grandma, Miss Agatha could be a new neighbor. Or it might be the name of a rose in her garden. Or a bird nesting in one of the birdhouses. Or a red squirrel living in one of the spruce trees at the edge of the woods.

Grandma talked about all living things like they were friends.

In this case, Miss Agatha was a cat.

Chapter 3

"Miss Agatha is a cat of mystery," Grandma said, carrying a bowl of cat food through the garden. "So I named her for Agatha Christie, the mystery writer."

I smiled. Lots of people wouldn't want a stray cat hanging around. But Mom always said that Grandma had "a soft heart." She could look at ordinary things and see something special.

I tried to follow without stepping on any flowers, but they were everywhere, even growing through the cracks in the walkway. At home in Ohio, Mom liked our yard to look neat, with just some bushes and trees around the edges. But I liked the bright, wild jumble of Grandma's yard. It was full of pathways and flower colors that don't usually go together: red and peach, purple and blue.

"It's so wrong that it's right!" Grandma liked to say.

"Where did Miss Agatha come from?" I asked.

"*That's* the mystery," Grandma said. "One day she just appeared at the edge of the woods. At first, I thought she belonged to the new family down at the Point. But then I met Cayman, and he said they didn't have any pets."

"Cayman?" I asked.

Grandma nodded. "He's about your age. He and his mom moved in last winter. I've told him all about you."

I clenched my teeth in a fake scared face. "What did you say about me?"

Grandma laughed. "The truth! I told him that you're perfect!"

I laughed with her, but inside, I felt weird that Grandma was talking to a boy about me.

"I posted Miss Agatha's photo on signs around town, but no one's claimed her," Grandma said. "So maybe she wandered away from her home and got lost. Or maybe someone abandoned her to fend for herself. But no matter how she got here, I won't let her go hungry."

At the edge of the garden, Grandma handed me the cat food. "Would you put this under the hydrangea bush? That's Miss Agatha's restaurant."

When I was little, I had a hideout under this huge hydrangea bush. Grandma would cut away the lowest branches so I had room to crawl underneath. It was my own secret leafy green room.

Now I barely fit.

I felt clumsy, crawling on my knees, one hand on the ground and the other sliding the bowl of cat food along.

"She won't come to me," Grandma said. "So I leave food for her every day, hoping she'll leave my songbirds alone."

I grimaced. Birds are my favorite animals, and I hadn't thought about Miss Agatha as a hunter. I left the bowl and crawled backward out from under the hydrangea. "Does it work?"

Grandma shook her head. "Not always. A cat will be a cat. So we must disagree about the songbirds."

Picking a dead hydrangea leaf out of my hair, I glanced over at a tiny yellow goldfinch perched on Grandma's bird feeder. It tossed aside a seed before choosing another to eat.

A few summers ago, one flew right at Grandma's kitchen window. I found it stunned and panting on the ground. When I picked it up, I could feel its tiny heart beating on my palm.

Grandma poked airholes in a box, and we left the gold-finch inside to see if it would recover. A few minutes later, we heard it fluttering in the box. When I opened the box flaps, the goldfinch flew away.

I cried when it was gone. I didn't even understand why. I wanted it to get well and be free. But then I felt empty when it was.

"Happy missing," Grandma called the feeling. It doesn't seem like *happy* and *missing* could go together, but sometimes they do.

I think I fell in love with birds that day. Grandma taught me to recognize some songs, and she sent me a bird feeder for Christmas. Maine and Ohio have some of the same birds, like goldfinches, blue jays, chickadees, wood-peckers, and cardinals. When those birds come to our yard at home, it always feels like a connection between Grandma and me.

The goldfinch at Grandma's feeder sang his happy song. I liked knowing which bird was talking and whether it was a happy song or a danger call or a threat of "Don't stop here! This is *my* home!" It was something most people didn't even listen to, but it comforted me and it gave me courage knowing there's a secret bird language happening all around, all the time. Full of danger, warnings, loneliness, and the joy of finding each other again.

And when they're quiet, that can mean something, too.

I looked back at Grandma's feeder, but the goldfinch was gone. Then I saw why. A dingy white cat was standing in the tall grasses at the edge of the woods.

Miss Agatha's gaze met mine. Watching me, she barely moved, just her tail flicked. I waited for her to look away first, but Miss Agatha was excellent at staring.

I looked hard at her. *Leave our birds alone. Go home where you belong.*

But where did she belong?

"We can watch Miss Agatha from the kitchen," Grandma said. "Let's *us* go have something to eat, too. It must be lunchtime by now. How about blueberry pancakes?"

"Okay." I wasn't hungry after the ice cream, but Grandma did make the best blueberry pancakes. I took a deep breath and let it go, still trying to relax and forget about everything happening at home.

"Bring the empty cat food can with you. We'll wash it and put it in the recycling," Grandma said. "The last step of any job—"

"Is cleaning up," I finished for her. "You always say that."

She laughed. "I guess I do."

As we rounded the corner of the house, I was surprised to see a boy coming up Grandma's driveway carrying a small plastic container. I'd met a lot of the kids who lived in Stone Harbor, but I didn't know him.

"Cayman!" Grandma called to the boy. "Come meet Mia, my beautiful granddaughter who I've told you so much about."

My face heated up. Only Grandma would call me beautiful, especially since Mom had woken me up at three a.m. to drive to the airport. I'd simply pulled back my brown hair into a ponytail and grabbed an old T-shirt and shorts that didn't even match, because my favorite clothes were all packed in my suitcase or in boxes.

The boy looked surprised to see me, too. He was about my age, wearing a long-sleeved flannel shirt and jeans, even though it was warm enough for shorts and a T-shirt. But the most striking thing about him was his blond hair down to his shoulders. He looked a bit wild and messy, but not like he cared.

"Cayman, you're just in time for lunch!" Grandma said.

"Oh. No thanks," Cayman said. "I just brought your container back."

Grandma tipped her head. "I'm making blueberry pancakes."

"Oh." He grinned. "Well, in that case, maybe I could stay a *little* while."

I smiled with them, even though I didn't feel it. I still felt edgy, like I hadn't settled in yet. And now she had company!

He'll go home after pancakes, I told myself.

"What would you like to drink, kids?" Grandma asked, holding the door open for Cayman and me. "I have orange juice in the fridge."

"I'll get it." I got the juice from the refrigerator. Then I turned to the cupboard for the glasses.

Cayman was already there. He took out three juice glasses.

He didn't have to ask or go looking—he knew right where to find them. Then he opened the silverware drawer and got out forks and knives.

I narrowed my eyes. *Who is this boy?* I wondered.

"Cayman, Mr. Holbrook said you can see the eaglets' heads above the nest now," Grandma said.

Cayman nodded. "They've really grown. I watched Rachel bring them a fish this morning."

"How magical! Would you like to go see them, Mouse?" Grandma asked.

I cringed. I wished she hadn't used that old nickname in front of him. It made me sound like a little kid. "Yes, I definitely want to go see the eagles. It's *our* special thing," I said, hoping Cayman would realize that meant he wasn't invited.

A walk with Grandma was exactly what I needed. I could tell her all about moving—the worries and doubts that I didn't want to share with Mom.

What if I didn't like my new room?

What if the new house came with a ghost?

What if the neighbors had a big, mean dog?

What if there were no kids my age in the new neighborhood?

And worst of all, what if moving made me forget the little memories of our old house? It's easier to forget things when you don't see them anymore. Like the burn mark on the kitchen floor always reminded me of the day Dad dropped a hot pan and rolls went everywhere. Or the scratch on the bathroom windowsill reminded me of the time Mom had to hoist me through the window when she locked us out of the house.

Mom had promised me I wouldn't have to change schools, but even so, I'd probably have to change buses. Would the kids on my new bus let me sit with them? How would I even know where the bus stop was?

And what if Scott realized that he didn't like living with a kid?

Grandma turned to Cayman. "Can I ask you a favor?"

"Sure," Cayman said. "Do you need me to reach something up high? Or load the trash cans into the car?"

"No," Grandma said, adding milk to the pancake batter. "Mia can help me with those things now that she's here."

I looked sideways at him. *Yes, I can.*

"I'd like you to take Mia to see the eagles," said Grandma.

Wait. What? "Aren't *you* coming?" I asked. "I thought we'd go together, like we always do." I hoped she couldn't hear how my voice was begging.

"Oh, I wish I could," Grandma said. "But the last time I went to the Point I twisted my knee climbing over those big rocks. It hurt for weeks, and my doctor scolded me good! You two go on without me. You'll get a much better view of those eaglets if you're not worrying about me."

"Um—" I couldn't think of a way to say that I didn't want to go with Cayman without sounding rude. "I don't want you to miss it."

"Oh, Mia. That's so sweet of you," Grandma said, stirring the pancake batter. "To be honest, it scared me a little to get hurt that day. You can say hi to the eagles for me. The path is right at Cayman's house. He can show you."

"I know where it is," I said.

Grandma had already turned to Cayman. "Stop back here when you're done. I'll have some supper for you to take home."

"That's okay," he said. "Mom said we might order pizza tonight."

"How nice!" Grandma said brightly. "I'll put it in a freezer container, then. You can save it for another night."

Listening to the sound of the pancakes sizzling in the pan, I felt annoyed that I'd been pushed off onto Cayman on my first day here.

He didn't look too happy, either.

I didn't want to hurt Grandma's feelings, though. And I did want to see the eagles at least once while I was here.

Really, how long could it take? An hour at the most? I looked up at the kitchen clock.

I could go and come back, and then Grandma and I could do everything else together.

"I'll say hi to the eagles for you and I'll take some photos," I offered. "That way you can see them, too."

"Perfect!" Grandma said.

It felt far from perfect to me. But as Dad liked to say, "Mia, don't worry so much about the little things."

This is one of those little things, I thought.

But I was wrong.

Chapter 4

Following Cayman along the path through the woods, I breathed in the smell of damp earth, pine needles, and spruce trees. It was every bit as wild and beautiful as I remembered.

A blue jay dipped his beak to drink from the tiny stream bubbling along the rocks in the woods. In some places, the moss was so thick that it looked like someone threw a velvety green blanket over the ground. Along the edges of the path, there were bushy ferns, starry white bunchberry flowers, and pink lady slippers. In other places, the trees were so close together and tall that they made me feel tiny, like a little kid trying to see between a bunch of adults' legs. I'd forgotten about the quiet, though.

When Mom and I hiked our town's nature trails, we always met someone walking their dog or taking photos or bringing their kids for a walk. You can't be alone for long there. It can be frustrating if I want to look for birds, but there's some comfort in it, too. If anything goes wrong, someone's bound to come along soon to help.

Stone Harbor could be quiet and isolated in a way that I almost never experienced at home. Here I heard mostly only nature sounds: the stream running over rocks, a far-off woodpecker drumming, branches moving high up in the breeze. It was people-quiet, except for Cayman's and my footsteps.

Now that it was just us, everything felt awkward. Each time I tried to talk to him, Cayman gave such short answers that there was nowhere for a conversation to go.

"Do you like living here?" I asked, trying again.

He shrugged. "It's okay."

"I love coming here," I said. "There's so much nature and people are so friendly. They wave to each other when they drive by."

"Maybe you wouldn't love it if you lived here all the time," he said flatly.

I looked sideways at him. He didn't have to say it like

that. Just because he lived here year-round didn't make his opinion matter more. "Maybe I *would*," I said.

It was hard for me to imagine Stone Harbor, my home away from home, as anything but a beautiful place full of pine trees, seabirds, seals, and people who said hi, even if they didn't know you. I honestly thought he was lucky to live here.

"My mom grew up here, and I've been coming here since I was born," I said. Cayman might live here every day, but I'd been coming longer. "Have you ever been to Ohio?" I asked.

He shook his head.

Then I knew some things he didn't! "Ohio is nice, too," I told him. "But in a different way than here. Where I live, everything is *much bigger*. There's a huge movie theater and lots of restaurants and stores. My school has six hundred kids and I don't even know them all! There's lots more diversity and choices than here. There is a much bigger range of things to do."

Cayman didn't look impressed enough yet, so I kept going. "For fun my friends and I like to go to an amusement park not too far away. And there's a community pool right down the road from my house."

A thought suddenly hit me. After the move, would the pool still be close enough for me to walk to?

"Well, the pool is close to my house *now*," I said. "We're moving, and I don't know exactly where the new house will be. But Mom promised I wouldn't have to change schools."

"Do you believe your mom?" Cayman asked.

"Of course!" What kind of question was that? Why wouldn't I believe her? "My mom wouldn't say it if it wasn't true!"

Cayman shrugged. "Sometimes things change."

"Not this," I said. "She knows it's important to me."

But inside, a tiny part of me got scared. Mom had promised, but what if there was a perfect house in another school district? Would she and Scott really say no?

The bend in the path was coming, and I slowed down to let Cayman go ahead of me. This path had always been special to me, and somehow he was ruining this walk. I looked down at my feet and took the steps around the bend alone. One, two, three, four, five—and there was sun on my sneakers.

Ahead, the light on the water sparkled so brightly that I had to look at the rocks to adjust my eyes. The eagles' nest was high in a tree farther down the shore. The only way to get there was to walk and climb over lots of big and little rocks: gray, black, tan, white, and even pink, all mixed together. Most of the little rocks were smoothed and rounded from the ocean passing over them between tides.

I was glad Grandma had made me change my flip-flops for sneakers. Even so, some rocks were extra slippery with piles of black-and-gold seaweed—covered in tiny bugs. Seaweed looks like clumps of ugly noodles out of the water, but underwater it's completely different. It shivers and waves like a cornfield back home when the breeze moves through it.

Cayman was way ahead of me now. Climbing over rocks, he knew exactly where to put his feet and hands.

I wished I hadn't taken Grandma's binoculars with me. It'd seemed like a good idea, but with them around my neck, they bumped into my chest over and over.

As I slid down a steep rock, Cayman's words kept coming to my mind. *Sometimes things change.*

I knew Mom would try to find a school in my school district. But I also knew lots of things were important to her and Scott. A short commute for them both, a nice neighborhood, at least two bathrooms—their wish list went on and on. Ken the Realtor told her to put a star by the most important things. I assumed Mom had starred my school district, but had she?

From the divorce, I'd learned sometimes things don't work out the way you want. Plans and even promises get changed sometimes.

Then *you* have to change.

I was so distracted that my foot slipped. I scratched my ankle on a sharp corner of granite. "Ouch!" I yelled. A trickle of blood slid down my ankle toward my sock.

Cayman came back to me. "Give me the binoculars," he said.

I didn't want to carry Grandma's binoculars anymore, but I didn't like the way he just *told* me he'd take them. "No, thank you," I said, smearing the blood away.

He shrugged. "Okay, but don't break the binoculars."

What an annoying boy! He didn't even ask if I was okay! As Cayman climbed ahead of me, I glared at the blond hair on the back of his head. If he looked back, I wanted him to see that I was mad at him. Maybe I'd even tell him to get a haircut if he wasn't going to bother combing it!

He didn't turn around, though. So I focused on finding dry, flat rocks to step on and crawl over. The gap between some rocks was so wide that I didn't dare jump it, like Cayman did. I sat down to get across, even though it put me farther behind him.

Finally, Cayman looked back. He sat on a rock and crossed his arms while he waited for me to catch up. "Why does your grandmother call you Mouse?"

I climbed past him, giving him a taste of the silent treatment. But then it felt too uncomfortable not to say something. "I was extra small when I was born," I told him.

I wasn't little anymore, but the nickname had stuck for a different reason. I used to be afraid of lots of things: thunderstorms, big dogs, slugs, pushy gulls, Disney villains, being lost, and people dressed up in furry costumes.

I was still afraid of some of those, just better at hiding it.

"Where'd *your* name come from?" I asked. "I've never known anyone named Cayman."

"I was named for the island where my dad came from," he said.

"Oh," I said, glad to finally know something interesting about him. "Have you ever been there?"

"No."

"Well, I'm glad *I'm* not named for the place that my dad came from," I said. "Because I'd be named Saskatchewan."

I saw the tiniest smile from him. "At least Cayman is easier to spell," he said, picking up a rock from the beach.

It wasn't much, but maybe the smile was a start. We didn't need to be forever friends, but it would be nice to get along, especially since Grandma liked him. "Do you have any pets?" I asked, because kids who *do* have pets usually like to talk about them.

He shook his head as he threw the stone, making it skip on a wave.

"Me either," I said. "I hoped I'd get a dog last year at my dad's, but I got a baby brother instead."

A long time ago, Dad promised me a dog when I was old enough to take care of it. But that was before the divorce, and a few months before, Dad and his new wife, Shelly, had Baby Luke.

Dad was busier now. I used to stay with him every weekend, but now with the baby, I spent one weekend a month. Which was okay with me because Luke didn't sleep through the night yet and I could see my friends on the weekends I was home. But sometimes when I called,

Dad snort-laughed when I wasn't saying funny things. I think he was watching Luke being cute. And Dad had to get off the phone quickly whenever Luke cried.

Dad hadn't mentioned a dog in a long time. "Well, if you *could* have a pet, what would it be?" I asked Cayman.

Cayman shrugged, skipping another stone. "A raven, maybe."

Okay, that was a more interesting answer than I'd expected. "Why a raven?"

"They're really smart," he said. "I read a book once about someone who had a raven as a pet. It learned how to do tricks and say 'Hello' and 'Wow' and 'Peanuts?' I wouldn't keep it in a cage, though. I'd want it to be free."

Was this why Grandma liked Cayman? She could talk birds with him when I wasn't there?

"Ravens have families, so it'd be mean to take a raven away from its family," I said to prove I knew about them, too. "But ravens and crows do remember people who've been nice to them. I read about a kid who left food for crows, and they left her some shiny things as a thank-you. You could try that. It wouldn't be a *pet*, really, but if you gave it things it liked, it might stick around. Like Miss Agatha does with Grandma."

Cayman shrugged. "Ravens are more independent than cats."

I nodded. "That's why if I could be any animal, I'd pick a bird. They do whatever they want and go wherever they want. They don't even need roads!"

"Birds don't really get to go *anywhere* they want," Cayman said. "Some birds have territories. Another bird might go there, but it can't stay."

I gave Cayman a side-eye. Did he always have to be right? Still, I was impressed a little bit. I didn't meet many kids who knew much about birds.

My phone chimed. One of Mom's phone rules was that I couldn't check my phone when I was spending time with someone. But I didn't think this really counted. Cayman and I didn't really *want* to be together.

"I'll catch up," I said.

The text was from Dad. **Hey, are you safely in Maine? I've been waiting to hear from you! Please text me ASAP to let me know you're okay!**

Oops. I was supposed to let him know when I'd arrived. He'd included Mom. I didn't want him to be upset with *her* for not letting him know.

I quickly replied to them both. **Yes! Hello from**

Maine! Sorry I got busy. Everything is great here. I fed Grandma's stray cat and she made pancakes. Now a boy is taking me to see the eaglets.

Mom would be more interested in the eagles than Dad, but sometimes it made problems if I told one parent something and not the other. They never actually said it hurt their feelings, but I could tell that it did. Dad would say, "No, I didn't know that. Maybe you told Mom?" and Mom just pinched her lips together, holding back words.

I loved them both, and I hated being in the middle. Even though there was nowhere else for me to be.

Dad texted back right away. **A boy?**

I rolled my eyes. **He's Grandma's neighbor. I told her I'd take a photo of the eaglets and the path is on his property.**

Dad replied, **Oh, okay! Glad to hear you're having fun and making friends!**

I looked over at Cayman skipping rocks into the water at the Point. *Fun* and *friends* weren't the words I'd choose.

But it wasn't worth explaining.

The Point was a fancy name for where the shoreline turned a corner. In one direction, there was a small island across a channel of water. The island was mostly bare rock, but there was a ragged group of pine and spruce trees at one end. A lobster boat was headed that way, the boat's wake looking like a twisted ribbon of water following behind it.

The other direction was open ocean. The waves were always bigger and the wind was stronger on that side. The wind had pruned the trees at the Point into odd shapes. At the top of the tallest spruce was a huge nest of sticks. Even without the binoculars, I could see two gray eaglet heads bobbing, their mouths open.

Rachel and HW's babies! I couldn't help grinning as I shot photos. Eaglets aren't graceful or fierce-looking, like their parents. They look like goofy, fuzzy baby-dinosaur puppets.

Above the nest, Rachel and HW were flying in wide circles. Female bald eagles are bigger than males, and that was the only way I could tell them apart. My heart swelled seeing them again. It was like seeing old friends.

Hi from Grandma and me! I said in my mind. Watching them, I thought it must be an amazing feeling to be that free. Flying wherever they wanted—

I glanced at Cayman. *Okay, okay. Flying wherever they wanted—except in another eagle's territory.*

Suddenly, one of the eagles screeched, sending a shiver between my shoulders.

I looked back to see them still circling, but that screech meant something was wrong.

"Are we too close?" I asked Cayman.

He shrugged. "*I've* been closer and they didn't complain."

I narrowed my eyes. Cayman made it sound like the eagles were upset about *me*. Even if that were true, he didn't need to say it.

If I get a few more photos for Grandma, I can leave, I promised myself. As I took the next photo, Rachel gave a piercing scream.

Just then, a big bird flew out of the tree next to the nest. It was about the size of the adult eagles, with yellow talons and a hooked beak. But it wasn't an eagle. This bird was white all over, not just on its head. It looked fierce and magical, like a bird from a fantasy book, not something real.

Rachel dive-bombed the white bird, feet first, her talons outstretched. She knocked the other bird sideways in the air.

I couldn't even breathe. Had Rachel hurt it?

The white bird didn't fall. It turned sharply. Pumping its wings hard, it flew straight upward—unlike any bird I'd ever seen—and it hit HW's chest hard from underneath. Rachel screamed as HW stumbled in the air.

I could barely breathe. "They'll kill each other!" I said. "We have to do something!"

"Hey!" Cayman jumped to his feet and waved his arms, yelling at them. "Hey!"

The white bird wheeled again. It went after Rachel this time. She took off, trying to outfly it.

My heart was pounding. "Hey!" I screamed with Cayman.

I thought the white bird would try to hurt Rachel, but it flew right past her! I wanted a photo to study later so I raised my phone to follow them. I wasn't sure if I could even get a photo, but I held my finger down for a burst and shot as many photos as possible.

The white bird flew across the channel, toward the island. Then all three birds disappeared behind the island's trees, the white bird ahead and the eagles chasing it.

My legs felt shaky, like they might not hold me up. "I've never seen anything like that," I said, leaning against a big rock so I wouldn't fall.

"Me either," Cayman said.

Now that the white bird was gone, it was hard to believe what I'd seen. This bird was too brave, too fierce, too willing to strike back to be any bird I knew. I wanted desperately for it to return.

In a weird way, it felt like it had come there just for me. That happens in books sometimes. A special sign appears in the sky or a magical being shows up, just when the main character needs it.

Cayman had been here plenty of times and had never seen it. So deep inside, I knew if it *was* a sign, it was for me. If I'd seen a vulture, I might have worried! But a magical white bird had to be a *good* thing.

Maybe our house wouldn't sell and we couldn't move. Or maybe we'd find a new house in the same neighborhood. So we'd move, but only down the street. And I wouldn't have to lose even more things that mattered to me.

Whatever the reason the bird had come, it was here and I felt braver, like it had loaned me some of its own strength.

Don't worry. I have enough fierce courage for both of us, I imagined it saying.

"We should go," Cayman said. "Rachel and HW need to take care of their babies. They may not come back while we're here."

I didn't want to leave, but we had been gone a long time. "Just give me a minute. Let me get a few more photos of the eaglets for Grandma."

All I could see were the eaglets' heads above the nest edge, but I shot photos from different angles, some zoomed in and some long shots with the ocean in the background.

I scrolled backward through my photos to be sure I had some good ones. I looked at photo after photo of the eaglets. Then I passed the last nest photo.

The next photo was blurry, but there it was.

A huge white bird chased by eagles.

Chapter 5

All the way home, I couldn't wait to show Grandma my photos of the white bird. I even ran up the driveway so I could tell her before Cayman did.

"You'll never guess what we saw!" I said, bursting into the kitchen.

Grandma looked up from the kitchen table, where she had the newspaper spread out to read. "The eaglets?"

"Yes, but also—" I was panting so hard from running that I had to take a deep breath.

"A big white bird," Cayman said behind me. "He upset Rachel and HW. They even fought with each other!"

I spun around. If my scraped ankle hadn't still hurt, I would've wanted to kick him for telling her before I could.

"Was it a gull?" Grandma asked. "Some black-backed gulls look huge, especially when they're flying."

I rolled my eyes. "I know what a *seagull* looks like. This bird had talons. It was definitely a raptor."

Cayman nodded. "It was bigger than an osprey and didn't have any brown. It was almost all white with some small black specks on its wings."

I hadn't noticed the black specks. I looked closely at the best photo I'd taken on my phone. As much as I hated to admit it, maybe Cayman was right. "Sorry it's small and blurry," I said, handing my phone to Grandma.

As Grandma looked closely, the lines between her eyebrows deepened. "Wow, look at that. Yes, it's a raptor for sure. The coloring reminds me of a snowy owl, but it's definitely not an owl." She smiled at me. "What a glorious find on your first day here! It must have heard you were coming!"

I smiled back, happy that Grandma thought like I did. It *was* special that the bird showed up the same day as me. "We both flew in," I joked.

"Maybe someone else has seen it and knows what it is," Cayman said. "I can ask around town."

"No," I said quickly. Somehow the bird felt like mine,

even though Cayman and I had seen it together. "I'll look it up on my phone."

I typed *big white raptor* into the search box and then added *Maine* to narrow it down.

I scrolled through photos of peregrine falcons, osprey, and eagles. "All of these birds have too much brown on them," I said when I reached the end of the list.

"Maybe it's leucistic," Grandma said.

"What's that?" I asked.

"It's a condition that happens with birds sometimes. Their feathers don't have as much pigment as usual," Grandma said. "I had a leucistic goldfinch here last winter. It was the most beautiful pale yellow—almost white. At first, I thought I had a new bird, but when I looked through the binoculars, it was definitely a goldfinch— simply a different color."

"Wow. I wish I could've seen that!" I said. "How do you spell it?"

"L-e-u-c-i-s-t-i-c," Grandma said.

I typed it into the search engine. The photos didn't even look real! There were white crows and eagles. Some had their typical markings, but the colors looked faded, lighter than usual. Other birds were completely white.

"Maybe that's it," I said, disappointed. I wanted to think it was magic, not science.

As I read about it, I felt extra disappointed that it was often a problem for the bird, not a good thing. A white bird in the summer didn't blend in as well, which left it open to predators.

Though our white bird seemed able to take care of itself.

"I'll ask Mrs. Wells at the library," Cayman said. "She knows a lot about birds. Email me the best photo you took, Mia."

I was tired of him telling me to do stuff. *Give me the binoculars. Email me the best photo you took.*

"I don't have your address," I stalled, going back to my search results. I clicked on a link for "Maine Birding Association."

Everything on the website was about birds: birding trips, information, links, and a message board. These people were experts! I quickly bookmarked the website to look at later.

"While you two were at the Point, I made macaroni and cheese," Grandma said, opening the freezer. "I have some for you to take home, Cayman. Just keep it in the freezer until you need it."

Need it? Didn't his mom cook?

He smiled in a teasing way. "I'll be sure to wash the container and bring it back," he said. "Because the last step of any job is cleaning up."

I couldn't believe it. That was my joke with Grandma! And he was about to take my bird away, too. I couldn't stop him from asking Mrs. Wells about it, but I could make it harder.

I opened a blank email. "Okay. What's your email address?" I asked.

Cayman stood there waiting, but I took my sweet time typing in his address and attaching a photo. "I'll warn you that it's not a great photo," I said, hitting Send.

Which was completely true.

I'd sent him the worst photo I'd taken.

Chapter 6

As soon as Cayman left, I showed Grandma the scratch on my ankle. "It's not a big deal, but I should probably clean it and put a Band-Aid on it."

Really, I had a plan. I knew Cayman would ask around town about the white bird, and I couldn't stand the thought of him coming up the driveway all proud and snooty with the answer tomorrow.

So I'd find out first. Even if it meant going over my limit on Mom's phone rules. As a scientist, she had to understand the importance of doing research.

As soon as I closed the bathroom door, I opened the Maine Birding Association website. The message board seemed like the best place to ask a question. I read through the headings: Birding Organizations, Just for

Fun, Attracting Birds to Your Yard, Bird Identification, For Sale, and Tips for New Birders.

I clicked on Bird Identification, but when I tried to post a message, a little box popped up.

You must create a profile to post.

My heart sank. Another of Mom's phone rules was that I couldn't give away any personal information online unless she approved it first.

But she was busy! She was traveling and then, when she got home, she'd be packing and painting. Who knew how long it would take for Mom to check this out and say okay?

Looking through the posts, I noticed something interesting. A few people used their real names, but most had chosen bird names.

Pelican.

GoldenEagle545.

RobinsEgg.

BlackScoter.

If I didn't use my real name, then I wasn't giving away personal information. As soon as I had an answer, I'd delete my profile.

It all seemed simple enough. And the more I thought

about it, the more I liked the idea of having a secret name. It could be my spy name! A secret other version of me.

I did a search for bird names that started with M.

Macaw—too fancy.

Mallard—too ordinary.

Mockingbird—too know-it-all.

Martin—too much like a boy's name.

Merlin—

The photo caption said a merlin was a small falcon. A raptor, just like the mysterious white bird. It felt like a nice mix: small like I used to be, but tough and brave, like I wanted to be.

I chose Merlin11 as a secret, spy version of me.

Finishing my profile, I knew I had to hurry. Too long in the bathroom might lead to embarrassing questions. I put a Band-Aid on my scratch while I thought about what I wanted to say.

Then I opened a new message and typed in the subject line: "Mystery Bird."

Hi. I took this photo today in Maine. Sorry it's not a better photo. I shot it with my phone. What is it?

I signed it "Merlin11" and included my best photo of the white bird.

As soon as I hit Submit, another little box popped up asking if I wanted to get a notification whenever someone responded to my post.

Why not? I shrugged and clicked Okay.

Grandma was getting two baskets from the cupboard above the refrigerator when I returned to the kitchen. "Would you like to help me pick some strawberries?"

"Sure!"

"Your mother always loved strawberries," Grandma said. "I have an old cookbook of my mother's and every year Beanie'd try a new recipe. Strawberry Buckle, Strawberry Crisp, Strawberry Grunt—"

"Strawberry Grunt? That sounds awful!" The only thing I remembered Mom ever making with strawberries was shortcake.

"It's like a cobbler, except you cook it on the stovetop," Grandma said. "You'd be surprised how tasty it is." She got out her recipe book. "Desserts are near the back."

The recipe book was old, a small notebook with a black leather cover. All the recipes inside were hand-written in cursive in blue ink. On some of the pages, there were stains. "Mom made a mess!" I said.

Grandma smiled. "Constantly experimenting. A scientist, even then."

"What else do you remember her cooking?" I asked.

"She always made birthday cakes for her friends," Grandma said. "She got very good at decorating them. Though I do remember the day Jenny Burnham's cake got dropped on the school-bus steps!"

"Oh no," I said. "Was it wrecked?"

"Well, it wasn't *pretty*," Grandma said. "But luckily the cake was in a box. So when Beanie got to school, she handed out forks and everyone ate it from the box."

I laughed. It was fun to imagine Mom as a kid making birthday cakes for her friends and testing out recipes. When I asked Mom about growing up in Stone Harbor, she mostly told me facts like what classes she liked in school (science, math, gym) and how she played basketball. That was why I loved Grandma's stories. They filled in the gaps between the facts.

I took a photo of the Strawberry Grunt recipe page to send to Mom. **You'll never believe what Grandma and I are making!** I texted.

I thought about sending it to Dad, too, but he wouldn't get the joke and it felt like a lot to explain. I knew I was above my screen time limit for the day, too. So I put my phone in my pocket to keep from being tempted.

Outside, I swung my basket past the rock wall next to the house. I felt better already. Grandma's garden was one of my favorite places. When I was little, it was a perfect spot to play, full of hideaways. Grandma didn't have many regular toys, so I played with whatever I could find, including the tokens from her board games.

The four gingerbread men from Candy Land had daring adventures. The iris leaves made dark jungles for them to explore and the mud became quicksand. The dog from Monopoly was their pet and had to rescue them when they were lost or stuck.

"Do you remember how I used to play with the Candy Land people?" I asked.

"Used to?" Grandma said. "You mean last year?"

I blushed, and I wasn't even sure why. It wasn't like Grandma cared if I still wanted to play. But I felt uncomfortable, too old for it now.

She smiled. "Last fall, I found a yellow gingerbread man in a clump of daylilies when the leaves died back."

"Oh, that's great!" I said. "I looked for him before I

left, but I guess I didn't look there. I was afraid maybe he was lost forever."

"Nope, he just spent the summer tending the day-lilies," Grandma said. "It was fun to find him, like you'd left me a little surprise."

Part of me did want to play with those tokens again, but I felt shy now thinking about other people walking by and maybe seeing me outside playing.

Especially Cayman.

"So how come Cayman spends so much time over here?" I didn't mean my words to come out like I was accusing her of something, but it did sound that way even to me. "I mean, he knew where the juice glasses were. And the forks!"

Grandma looked surprised at my reaction. "He stops by sometimes," she said, shrugging. "He's a big help when I need it, and it's nice to have his company. He's a good kid, just a little lonely. I'm glad you met him. He needs friends his age. Not just old ladies."

"You're not old!" I said, kneeling in the strawberry patch. Strawberries grow low to the ground and sometimes you have to move the leaves to see the red berries.

"Why would you think I was talking about me?" Grandma asked.

I flinched, but she laughed. "Of course I was talking about me! I'm teasing you."

I smiled with her. Pinching a strawberry stem between my index finger and thumbnail, I twisted and pulled, letting the berry roll onto my palm. I didn't want to feel jealous of Cayman, but I couldn't help it. Grandma was the one person I didn't expect to share. Mom had Scott, Dad had Shelly and Baby Luke. And with each new person who got added, it felt like my piece of Mom and Dad got smaller.

I couldn't stand the idea of it happening with Grandma, too. Especially not because of some boy who didn't even seem to like me!

Careful not to squish the strawberry, I set it in my basket. "I don't mind spending *a little* time with him, but I really want to spend time with you."

She nodded. "Me too. As soon as I heard you were coming, I started counting the days! And today, I counted the hours. I couldn't wait for you to get here."

I twisted another red strawberry off the plant. As I set it into the basket, my phone chimed in my pocket.

"What's that sound?" Grandma asked.

"It's just my phone," I said.

"I promised your mother I wouldn't let you forget her phone rules," Grandma said. "So I'm trusting you to keep track of them. Okay? I don't want her and Scott to decide you can't come here by yourself again."

I nodded. "Don't worry. The text is probably *from* Mom! I bet she got my text about making Strawberry Grunt. Or maybe they're at the airport. I'd better check in case she needs something, though."

My phone chimed again, even as I was taking it out of my pocket.

I had two alerts from the birding group.

"Tell Beanie I said hi," Grandma said, picking another strawberry.

I felt guilty letting her think it was Mom. But I could say hi next time Mom texted. Then I wouldn't be lying. It'd just be a difference in *timing*.

I muted my phone to keep it from making any more sounds and opened the message board. Under my message were several replies. Even as I started reading them, more were appearing!

Peregrine? Definitely a falcon. —Screecher

Wrong coloring for a peregrine unless leucistic? —Sparrows4me

Too big for a peregrine. Look at the size in relation to the eagle. —BirdingBen

Maybe the eagle is smaller than usual? Of course it's hard to tell in a cell phone photo. —Screecher

Merlin11, you have given us a good mystery. If this bird is still hanging around, could you take a better photo? —BirdingBen

All my excitement deflated with a long breath. Even the birders weren't sure! But at least they thought it was special, too.

If you don't have a camera, you can try holding your phone up to the lens of your binoculars. —Swannie

Or you could ask someone with a great camera to join you! I'd volunteer! —BirdingBen

Inviting a stranger to join me was *definitely* not okay with Mom's phone rules. I sighed and closed the message board.

"I think we have enough now," Grandma said.

I looked at her basket full of strawberries and my almost-empty one. I couldn't believe I'd let myself get so involved reading messages that I missed out on something fun with Grandma. "I'm really sorry. I got distracted."

"That's okay," she said. "Let's eat yours and save mine for cooking." She grinned. "And tell Beanie to follow her own phone rules!"

I swallowed hard. *I won't let this happen again*, I promised myself.

We both chose a strawberry from my basket. Mine tasted warm and sweet, like summer in my mouth.

When Grandma smiled at me, her teeth were red with juice. "You have strawberry teeth," I teased her.

"So do you!" she said.

I turned my phone completely off so it wouldn't distract me anymore.

Chapter 7

The next morning, Grandma told me she had a breakfast meeting for the Stone Harbor Garden Club. "It's a big day. We're deciding what color petunias and geraniums to plant around the memorial for Stone Harbor fishermen lost at sea. Do you want to come?"

I giggled. "That takes a whole meeting?"

"Oh yes!" Grandma said, looking through her purse for her car keys. "There's sure to be an argument!"

I hated to miss the excitement! But I was anxious to try the idea that Swannie on the message board had suggested of using binoculars with my phone to take a closer photo. And even if my white bird had flown away by now, I might get some better photos of the eaglets that way.

"Do you mind if I stay here?" I asked. "I have a photo

idea I want to try. But if you want my opinion, I think purple petunias and white geraniums would look nice."

"Yes, I like a daring choice!" Grandma said, pulling her car keys out of her purse. "Maybe even purple with pink! The red-geranium-white-petunia group are sure to put up a fight, though. They always do."

"Good luck!" I said.

"I'll need it," Grandma said, walking out the door. "See you sometime around lunch."

At home, Mom would've had to give her usual instructions before she left. Like "If you need help, call me," and "Don't let anyone in until I get back." She would've said exactly when she'd be home, too. I loved that Grandma just trusted me to know what to do myself. It made me feel older and responsible.

As soon as she was gone, I got her binoculars and pulled one of her lawn chairs to a spot near the bird feeders.

I waited for some birds to come so I could practice. But the only bird around was a chickadee somewhere up in the trees giving its warning call, *chicka-dee-dee-dee-dee*. The number of *dee*s tells how big the danger is. The more *dee*s, the more trouble.

Then I saw *why* the chickadee was warning. Miss Agatha was lying in the sun at the far end of the garden.

Perfect! I placed the phone's camera lens against the binocular lens. Nothing showed on my phone screen— just black—so I held the binoculars still and moved the camera a tiny bit at a time, trying to line up the lenses.

Suddenly, light appeared on the screen. Then a circle full of green leaves and purple flowers, like looking at the garden through a porthole window. Miss Agatha wasn't in the circle, so I moved the camera and binoculars together. It was a slow process, because one little bobble and I had to start over.

Miss Agatha's tail appeared in the circle first. Then her body. *Just a tiny bit to the left.*

Finally, I had her face on the screen. She was a pretty cat, bigger than I thought.

But I was using both hands to hold the binoculars and phone. How could I push the button to take a photo? *Could I push it with my nose?*

I moved my face closer to my phone.

"What are you doing?" a voice asked behind me.

I startled, bumping my phone, losing the image on the

screen. Cayman was standing there, holding Grandma's macaroni-and-cheese dish, all clean. "Why were you kissing your phone?" he asked.

"I wasn't!"

"It looked like you were," he said, raising one eyebrow.

"Well, then you're wrong!" I could feel myself blushing, though. "Someone told me if you hold your phone lens and the binocular lens together, it'll act like an extra zoom. So I wanted to try it. But then I couldn't push the button because my hands were busy. So I was using my nose."

He leaned over to see. "Did it work?"

I looked at the photo my nose had taken. It was all black, no Miss Agatha at all. "No. What I need is a third hand."

"I could push the button for you," Cayman said.

He looked sincere, and I didn't have another option. "All right," I said. "But wait until I tell you I'm ready."

Cayman got behind me, and I put the camera's lens against the binoculars. I moved my phone slowly until they were lined up.

This time when Miss Agatha appeared on the screen,

I could even see her yellow-green eyes staring at me.

"Now!" I said.

From the corner of my eye, I saw Cayman's index finger coming. *Don't move. Don't move*, I told myself, trying to keep my hands steady.

He touched my phone.

The photo was blurry, but at least Miss Agatha was in it.

"Better," I said. "Can we try again? I think this'll take some practice."

"And luck," Cayman said. "Your grandma planted catnip over there for her. That's why she likes that spot."

"Shh. I'm concentrating!" I didn't like him knowing things about Grandma that I didn't. I hadn't meant to say that so sharply, though. "Sorry. This is just hard. Okay, push the button."

Cayman touched it gently. "Got it!"

This time the photo had better focus. Maybe this would really work. "I thought I'd try this with the eaglets today," I said.

His eyebrows went up. "Wow. That'll be harder. In fact, everything would have to go right for it to work. And—"

"And maybe things *will* go right!" I said. "I want to try, even if it's hard. If you don't want to come, that's fine. But can I cross your property to get to the path?"

Cayman paused. "I didn't say I didn't want to come," he said. "And you need a third hand."

I rolled my eyes. *Mr. Right Again.*

"Do you think the white bird will still be there?" Cayman asked.

"I don't know. I hope so!" I braced myself to hear him gloat and tell me what kind of bird it was. As the seconds went by and he didn't say anything, I couldn't stand it. If he'd found out before me, I wanted to get it over with. "So did you find out what kind of bird it is?"

"No, my mom wasn't feeling well yesterday when I got home," Cayman said. "So I didn't go out."

"Oh." I didn't want his mom to be sick, but I was glad he didn't get to show off. "I hope she feels better."

He smiled. "Thanks. What time do you want to meet up?"

"I just have to wait until Grandma gets back," I said. "She's at a petunia meeting. Apparently, it's a big deal what color flowers get planted around the fishermen's memorial. She'll be back around lunchtime. Is that a good time?"

He nodded, handing me the macaroni-and-cheese container. "See you then."

Watching him walk away, I was surprised to feel okay that he'd be coming with me. Cayman was annoying and bossy, but it was nice to have another kid to do a few things with—especially one who liked birds as much as I did.

When Grandma got home, I asked what the garden club had decided. "Did you convince them to try purple?"

Grandma shook her head. "Purple didn't stand a chance against the red-and-white team. I don't know why they like doing things the same way all the time. I wish they'd try something new! Make a change! Be bold!"

I understood, though. "Change is hard sometimes, I guess."

"Are you okay?" Grandma asked. "You look sad all of a sudden."

"Oh," I said. "I was just thinking about home. I'm worried about the new house."

"What are you worried about?" Grandma asked.

"Do you think there might be a ghost? Or a scary dog that lives next door? Or a neighbor who hates kids?"

I asked, everything coming out in a rush. "Or what if there isn't a good house in my school district and we have to live somewhere else? Mom promised, but what if there just *isn't* a good house in the right place?"

"Whoa! That's a lot of worries." She smiled kindly at me. "Even if things aren't perfect, I have complete faith in you, Mia. You're smart and capable. You'll figure it out as you go."

That didn't feel satisfying. And I couldn't even bring myself to ask her about my most secret worries, like forgetting things about when Mom, Dad, and I lived in our old house together. Or what if Scott decided he didn't like living with a kid? Or what if everything simply went wrong and couldn't be fixed?

Grandma put her arm around me. "Let's do something fun today. What do you think? It's a nice day for miniature golf."

Normally, I'd jump at the chance. "I really do want to go, but maybe we could go another day? I just asked Cayman if he'd help me with something. He's expecting me to come over."

She nodded. "Of course! We have lots of time. Go have fun with Cayman."

I tried to push away my worries. "I have a plan to get some good photos of the eaglets for you. I'm not sure it'll work, but I want to try it." I didn't mention hoping that the white bird was still around and I could get a better photo of it. There were so many things I wanted to find out. What was it? Where had it come from? Was it a magical bird or a real one?

Cayman wasn't outside when I got to his house. So I climbed the porch steps and knocked softly on the front door. I felt silly standing there. Grandma had insisted I wear her straw hat to keep from getting sunburned and her binoculars were around my neck. It looked like I was dressed up as a bird-watcher for Halloween.

The woman who answered was younger than Mom, but her eyes had dark circles under them and her blond ponytail was coming undone. This had to be Cayman's mom. Cayman said she'd been sick. Had I woken her up?

"Oh, I'm sorry to bother you," I said. "I'm Mia. Is Cayman here?"

He appeared in the doorway behind her. "I'll be down at the Point, Mom." He grabbed a sweatshirt from beside the door. "Will you be okay?"

"Of course," she said flatly.

I opened my mouth to say goodbye to his mom, but she was shutting the door.

"Okay, bye," I said to the door.

Cayman was already headed down the path, without even checking if I was coming.

Something didn't feel right. Maybe I'd shown up while Cayman and his mom were in the middle of something hard, like before the divorce when I'd come into the room while Mom and Dad were fighting. They'd suddenly notice me and say something normal, like nothing was wrong. But their cheerful words didn't match their upset eyes.

I hadn't heard Cayman and his mom arguing when I arrived, but it felt the same. Like things didn't match.

Part of me wanted to ask him, but I wasn't brave enough.

When we got to the shore this time, I watched where Cayman placed his hands and feet—which rocks he stepped on and which he stepped over. I jumped across cracks that he jumped across and held on where he held on. I didn't sit down to scoot once.

Cayman barely said a word to me, except "Give me the binoculars so you don't break them."

Always talking like he was the boss! But when I opened my mouth to say no, I knew it *would* be easier to climb over the big rocks without them. "Be careful with them," I said so he'd know that I didn't think he was perfect, either.

Climbing over the flat rocks, I made sure not to put my hands on the sharp barnacles or broken crab and clam shells that the gulls had dropped, trying to break them open. Cayman and I climbed in silence, to only the sound of a lobster boat's engine pulsing as it drove from trap to trap out near the island.

As the Point came into view, I saw HW and Rachel at the nest feeding the eaglets.

I sighed, my hopes deflating. They wouldn't look so relaxed if the white bird were around. Maybe it was even gone for good.

"I think we should stop here," Cayman said. "We don't want to scare Rachel and HW while they're feeding the babies."

"You don't have to tell me," I said, irritated. "I know how close to get."

At least I could take some great photos of the eaglets for Grandma. I found a good sitting spot. I put the camera against the binocular lens.

"Take your time," Cayman said, balancing one small rock on top of another. "The eaglets can't fly yet. They aren't going anywhere."

I adjusted and readjusted the binoculars and camera. It seemed to take forever for me to get everything lined up. Cayman built a tiny cairn of rocks waiting for me.

Finally, I saw some sticks. The nest! I moved everything up a little.

An eaglet's head appeared on my screen. I could even see its curved beak! It looked scary sharp—even on a baby.

"I'm almost ready." I moved slightly to get both eaglets in the shot. HW was perched on the edge of the nest, too. As Cayman got behind me, I held my breath waiting for Rachel to lean down to feed the eaglets. Then they'd all be in the photo.

"Now!" I whispered.

Cayman reached his arm over my shoulder to touch the button. When I looked at the photo, there was Rachel feeding an eaglet! It wasn't in perfect focus and I didn't get both eaglets or HW, but it was the best photo I'd taken so far.

"Grandma will love it!" I said. "It's cool that the binoculars make a circle frame for the photo, too. I think it looks like the porthole of a ship. Or maybe—"

Cayman grabbed my shoulder.

"Ouch!" I said. "What—"

"It's back!" he said in my ear. "Quick, line up the lenses. Before the eagles see it!"

I looked up. On a branch above us, my white bird was watching the eaglets.

I couldn't do anything fast enough, though. It was like I was moving through water. Line up the camera and binocular lens. Lift them together.

No way is this going to work, I thought.

My hands were shaking, making it harder than ever to keep the lenses together. On the screen, I could only see pine needles.

"Hurry," Cayman said.

"I can't!" I said. "Hurrying only makes it worse!"

As I moved the lenses to the left, an eagle screeched.

"Rachel has seen it," Cayman said. "Hurry up!"

"I'm doing the best I can!"

And suddenly, I had the white bird on my screen.

It was magnificent—that was the only word I could think of. Something so far from ordinary that it seemed from another world.

The bird tilted its head to the side to look at me with its dark eye.

You came back to me, I told it in my mind.

Cayman's hand came into the side of my view, but I didn't take my eyes off my phone screen. This bird wasn't a leucistic eagle. It wasn't the same shape as Rachel and HW at all.

Rachel screeched again. The white bird raised its wings.

Oh no! Don't fly! Not yet!

As it lifted off the branch, I let my shoulders drop. I couldn't possibly line up everything fast enough again to shoot a flying bird.

I watched the white bird lead the eagles away across the channel and tried to take a picture with my mind to remember it forever.

As the birds disappeared on the other side of the island, Cayman said, "Wow. Let me see the photo."

"I didn't get one," I said sadly. "It happened too fast."

"But I pushed the button," he said.

I hadn't even noticed. When I looked at my phone, a shiver shot up my back.

White feathers with a few black speckles. A fierce hooked beak and dark eye. Wings raised almost in flight.

We got the shot.

Chapter 8

I ran all the way to Grandma's, even though there was no chance of me being second. Cayman hadn't even come back with me.

"You won't . . . believe it!" I told Grandma, so out of breath that the words rushed out in clumps. "I tried that trick . . . of using . . . the camera and the binoculars . . . together. Cayman had to help me . . . because it took . . . three hands."

"Slow down, slow down," Grandma said. "Take a deep breath."

"Look!" I showed Grandma my photo.

Her eyes widened. "Oh my goodness! What a lovely creature. I've never seen a bird like it." She smiled. "It's a bird of mystery!"

"Maybe it's a mystery where it came from," I said. "But now with this photo, I bet we can find out what kind of bird it is."

"Yes! I'm sure the library has some bird books," Grandma said. "We can look it up!"

I had a different idea. I didn't think Grandma's tiny town library would have a book that showed my bird. The Stone Harbor Library was the kind of library that was fun to browse in, but it didn't have books about *everything*. Not like my big library at home with two elevators, four floors of books, lots of librarians, and a huge parking lot.

In fact, if Grandma's town library didn't have a sign out front, you'd think it was someone's house—because a long time ago, it was! The library was a white house with black shutters. It had a long front porch with a few rocking chairs and a TOWN HAPPENINGS! bulletin board.

It would be fun to spend time with Grandma and visit the library, though.

"I have a few things to donate to the church rummage sale," Grandma said. "Do you mind if we drop those off on the way to the library?"

"That's fine," I said.

While Grandma was getting the box of rummage sale donations, I pulled out my phone. I wouldn't let my phone get in the way of spending time with Grandma today. But I was sure I could get a quick answer while she was busy.

I quickly posted a new message on the birding message board.

The white bird is still there. It's hanging around near the bald eagles' nest. Thanks for the idea to use the camera lens and binoculars together.

I attached the photo and hit Submit.

Now all I had to do was wait!

And I didn't wait long. On the walk into town, my phone vibrated in my pocket. If I hadn't been carrying a box for the rummage sale, I would've been tempted to sneak a peek.

But I knew that once we got to the church, Grandma would chat with the other ladies awhile. Then I could check my phone.

Even so, knowing I had a message and not reading it was like having an itch I couldn't reach. Knowing you can't scratch it doesn't stop it from itching.

As I passed Holbrook's, my phone vibrated again. Now the itch to check it was worse, more like a fiery mosquito bite. I walked faster.

The Stone Harbor Community Church was a simple white church with a big bell below the steeple. At home, we didn't go to church, but when we visited Grandma, we did. I'd been to Sunday services, bean suppers, and I'd even been baptized there, though I didn't remember it.

The rummage sale was always a big fundraiser for the church and a chance for people to sell their old things. In the room below the sanctuary, ladies were busy sticking price tags on dishes, clothes, and old toys.

It looked like a thrift store had exploded.

"We've brought you some treasures and some junk!" Grandma said. "You can decide which is which!"

I set the box down on the only empty spot I could find on one of the tables. Mrs. Holbrook came over and hugged me. "My husband said he'd seen you at the store! Good to have you back, Mia!"

"That can't be Beanie's girl?" another lady asked.

"Oh, I remember her as such a little thing," another one said. "She's quite the young lady now!"

I forced a smile. Visiting Stone Harbor always felt like seeing a bunch of relatives who knew me more than I knew them. It was a weird mix of uncomfortable and nice. The uncomfortable part was being talked about and hugged by someone you rarely saw and hardly knew. But the nice part was belonging without having to do anything except show up.

"Mia, go ahead and look around," Grandma said. "If you see something you like, I'll buy it for you."

I felt too old for the toys and too young for the dishes. But looking around gave Grandma an excuse to chat and me a chance to check my phone. I pretended to be very interested in the coffee mugs.

I checked my messages while Grandma was busy asking about a bottle drive for the town school. Mom had sent me that photo of my bookcase like she'd promised, but the rest were from the birding message board.

WOW! WOW! WOW! It's a white gyrfalcon for sure! What a find! —BirdingBen

A gyrfalcon? I'd never heard of that, but I liked the sound of it. Although it was a real bird, it still sounded like a creature from a fantasy book.

Lucky capture! Gyrfalcons are arctic birds. Most often gray—in fact, I usually only see white gyrs in Greenland! —IcelandicGull

Not unheard of in Maine, but rare and a mega rarity in summer. —BirdingBen

Not just "rare," but "a mega rarity"! My heart was racing as more notifications from the message board popped up. They were coming so fast I could barely keep up.

Could it belong to a falconer? I don't see any gaiters, though. —Swannie

Maybe it was looking for territory and took a wrong turn. Or got blown off course in a storm. —Screecher

"Well, I'd invite her, but she mostly keeps to herself! She doesn't seem interested in talking to anyone." I heard a woman complain. "Kind of suspicious, if you ask me."

"Now, Missy, she has a nice boy," Grandma said. "That's what *I* know for sure. The rest is just gossip."

I turned to look at them, because the conversation sounded much more interesting than the school bottle drive now.

"Oh, Mia," Grandma said brightly. "Did you find something you like?"

I looked back quickly at the table of dishes. It seemed rude to admit there was nothing I wanted. So I picked out a pretty bowl with purple violets on it. "Maybe this can be for Miss Agatha?"

"Splendid idea!" Grandma said, getting out her money. "Even a stray cat deserves some fancy things."

"You put that money away!" Mrs. Holbrook said. "Just take it!"

"How will the church make money with you giving things away?" Grandma protested, but Mrs. Holbrook insisted. It seemed silly to argue over fifty cents, but it gave me a last chance to look at my phone.

Hard to believe this photo is real. I think you all are being played. —Razorbill207

The smile slid off my face. How dare Razorbill207 say that? I wasn't making it up! He didn't even know me!

I sent a quick reply.

It is real. I've seen it twice now.

Where? —Razorbill207

"Are you ready?" Grandma asked.

I startled. I hadn't even noticed that she'd finished chatting. She was holding the dish for Miss Agatha in one hand and the outside door open for me with the other. I nodded and held up one finger. *One minute!*

Mom had said I could never give my address online. And I definitely would never do that. I didn't have to be exact, though.

Stone Harbor.

Chapter 9

On the walk to the library, I couldn't wait to share my news. "I have a surprise!" I told Grandma. "I know what the white bird is! It's called a gyrfalcon, and it usually lives in the Arctic. It's a mega rarity in Maine."

"A gyrfalcon? Wow! I've never even heard of that!" Grandma said. "How on earth did you find out?"

"I learned about it online." Then, before Grandma could bring up my phone rules, I added, "Let's still go to the library, though. We can pick a book to read together."

When I was little, Grandma read to me every night. Now we took turns reading aloud, curled up on Grandma's couch.

"Great idea!" Grandma said. "And you can tell Mrs. Wells about the gyrfalcon. She loves birds!"

I paused. It would be fun to tell the librarian about it. But I had a weird feeling in my stomach. The gyrfalcon felt like mine, a secret I shared just with Cayman and Grandma. Did I really want to share it with anyone else? It was one thing to tell the people online. They lived somewhere else, and I didn't even know their real names. It was something different to tell people that I knew in town.

Just outside the library, Grandma showed me the flyer she'd made for Miss Agatha. It was hanging on the TOWN HAPPENINGS! bulletin board.

FOUND CAT!

IF YOU'RE MISSING A BIG WHITE CAT, SHE'S HANGING AROUND MY BIRD FEEDERS!

Grandma had signed it and included her phone number.

"Did anyone call?" I asked.

She shook her head. "I hate to think someone abandoned Miss Agatha. But the longer it takes for someone to claim her, the more I worry that no one's looking for her."

I felt a rush of pity for Miss Agatha. Even though our situations were different, I knew how hard it was to have your life turned upside down. At least I knew why things had changed, and the people I loved didn't just disappear, like hers had.

For the first time, I felt a connection to Miss Agatha. Just like me, she was facing new things and needed Grandma to help her.

As Grandma held the library door open for me, I gave her a quick hug. "Oh! What's that for?" she asked, grinning.

"Just for being you," I said.

Stepping across the doorway to the library, I took in a deep breath smelling of old books. I loved the Stone Harbor Library, even though it was the smallest library I'd ever been inside.

Mrs. Wells looked up from her big desk and grinned. "Hello, Mia! How nice to see you! Are you here with Beanie?"

Mrs. Wells had been the librarian for years. She went to school with Mom and had known me since I was born.

"Nope. Just me!" I said. "Mom's getting our house ready to sell, so I came by myself. She and Scott are buying a new house."

"What a fun adventure!" Mrs. Wells said. "Please tell your mom I said hi."

I took out my phone. "I'll send her a photo of us. I know she'd like that."

Grandma, Mrs. Wells, and I squeezed in together so I could get us all in the photo.

We're at the library! Mrs. Wells says hi! I'm having fun. I hope you are, too! I texted. Even though Mrs. Wells was Mom's friend more than Dad's, I sent the photo to them both.

Dad immediately sent back a photo of Baby Luke chewing on a toy. **Glad to hear it's going so well! Please say hi back to Mrs. Wells!**

Mrs. Wells hadn't really said hi to *him*, but no need to say so. Though Dad had come to Stone Harbor plenty of times with Mom, the town automatically took her side when they divorced.

As I slipped my phone back into my pocket, Grandma said, "We've come to the library on a mission! We need some information."

"You've come to the right place," Mrs. Wells said. "If I don't know the answer, I usually know where to look. What can I help you with?"

I paused, but there was no turning back now. Since I had to tell her, it would be fun to see Mrs. Wells's reaction. "Do you have any books about gyrfalcons?" I asked, watching her face. "They're falcons that *usually* live in the Arctic."

"Gyrfalcons? Hmm." Mrs. Wells got up from her chair and headed between the bookshelves. "Let's see what we can find!"

"She didn't even ask why," I whispered to Grandma. "Or seem surprised."

"It takes a lot to surprise a librarian," Grandma said. "They hear it all."

"Whatever books we have would be right here," Mrs. Wells said, running her hand along the spines. "Birding is a popular hobby, so we have quite a few books about Maine birds and especially the common birds that you'd find in your backyard. But gyrfalcons wouldn't be included in those."

Grandma grinned at me. "Perhaps they should be!"

I nodded. "At least in Stone Harbor."

Mrs. Wells looked back at us, surprised.

Grandma and I laughed, and then Grandma explained why. "I was telling Mia that you hear it all and it takes a lot to surprise you."

"I *am* surprised and curious!" Mrs. Wells said.

I took out my phone. "Cayman and I saw this bird at the Point. Some experts on a birding website said it's a gyrfalcon."

As Mrs. Wells looked at my best photo, her mouth dropped open. "Oh! Look at that!" she said. "Yes, you have definitely surprised me! What an exquisite bird. You saw this at the Point?"

I nodded. "It showed up the day I arrived. We flew in together."

Mrs. Wells smiled at my joke.

"It might not still be there," I said. "Rachel and HW keep chasing it off."

Mrs. Wells nodded. "I imagine they're protecting their nest. Since the eaglets can't fly yet, they'd be an easy meal."

My excitement drained out of me. I hadn't thought about *why* the gyrfalcon was hanging around the nest or why Rachel and HW were so mad at it.

"Don't worry, Mouse. Eagles know how to protect their babies," Grandma said, then sighed. "But people here do love those eagles. Rachel and HW are practically celebrities. It might be upsetting to know there was another raptor hunting around the nest."

Mrs. Wells nodded. "Some people might even want to remove the gyrfalcon to protect the eaglets."

Remove it? Suddenly, I felt afraid. I didn't want to ask *how* they might remove it. At home when people got upset with wildlife, they did something about it. And it usually resulted in something bad for the animal.

For pesky skunks and raccoons, they might hire someone to trap and relocate them. Which sounds kind, except most animals die when they're suddenly dropped off far from home with no idea where to find food or water. Or for pigeons, they put spikes on their windowsills to keep them from resting there. For some animals, there wasn't even a law against killing them.

"Can we keep this a secret?" I asked. "I don't want anyone to be angry at the gyrfalcon and maybe hurt it."

"Yes, I think it'd be for the best," Grandma said.

Mrs. Wells nodded. "We'll keep it between us. The fewer people who know the gyrfalcon is here, the better."

That was the plan, anyway.

That night, Grandma and I sat together on the couch. It felt wonderful to be just the two of us as we took turns reading aloud interesting facts about gyrfalcons from the birding books.

The bird's name is pronounced "JER-falcon."

Gyrfalcons are the largest falcons in the world.

Females weigh more than males.

Their legs are fully feathered.

Gyrfalcons can average 50–68 mph in level flight.

Gyrfalcons make various sounds. They chup, chatter, wail, whine, and have two alarm calls (kak-kak-kak and kikikkikkiki).

Their colors can vary from pure white with black speckles to dark gray.

In the Middle Ages, only royalty could own a white gyrfalcon.

My own gyrfalcon was wild, not owned by anyone. But still it felt like mine, because it had arrived with me. It had looked right at me. And now I was going to protect it from harm. I didn't know how, exactly, but I was willing to do whatever it took.

That brave feeling lasted until I heard the first rumble of thunder. Storms blow in fast near the ocean. Sometimes they arrive with just a growl of warning and sometimes with no warning at all, like the sky just suddenly turns dark and explodes with lightning.

"Shut the windows upstairs for me?" Grandma asked. "I'll get the downstairs ones."

Racing up the stairs, I thought about the gyrfalcon. Living in the Arctic, it was probably used to scary weather. Still, I hoped it would find somewhere safe to ride out the storm.

As I shut the first window, lightning flashed. I trembled as the thunder boomed behind it. Grandma always said the closer the flash and the boom were together, the closer the lightning was. I raced through shutting windows so I could run back downstairs to Grandma.

Suddenly, I wished I were home. I missed Mom. I missed my room. I missed everything around me feeling familiar and safe.

"Are you scared? You're shaking like a leaf," Grandma said when she saw me.

I couldn't even answer. My throat felt like it had a ball stuck in it. So I just nodded.

Grandma put her arms around me. "Well, some things are worth being careful with. Lightning is one of them. But as long as you're safe inside, storms can be beautiful. Don't you think?"

I shook my head.

"Have I ever showed you a storm from the attic?" she asked.

I felt ready to pass out. "Why would you do that?"

"Because it's something you'll never forget," Grandma said. "I'm going up. Are you brave enough to come with me?"

I wasn't, but I wasn't brave enough to stay downstairs alone, either.

As Grandma started upstairs, I hurried after her. She talked to me the whole way to the second floor, and then up the steep, narrow attic stairs. I couldn't really pay attention to what she was saying, though. All I could think about was how we'd be closer to the lightning in the attic and that seemed like a bad idea.

Grandma's attic was spooky enough in the daylight, but in the thunderstorm's weird yellow light, all the boxes and trunks looked like places for creepy things to hide. Grandma pulled two milk crates over near the window.

She sat on one.

I stared at the other. "You're not supposed to be near the window during a thunderstorm."

"The storm's not close," Grandma said. "It's over the ocean."

"Are you sure?" I asked.

"Come see for yourself."

I stood behind the milk crate and looked out the window.

A bolt of lightning flashed way out at sea. Then another, even farther away. A few seconds later, one struck close enough to light up the harbor for a second.

One after another, the bolts flashed at different distances, like a laser light show with loud and soft thunder.

Miles and miles of lightning strikes over the water.

Grandma was right that I'd never seen anything like it. It was terrifying and beautiful at the same time.

"How long will it last?" I asked.

"As long as it wants," she said. "Do you want to sleep with me tonight, Mouse?"

I wanted to be brave and say "No thank you. I'm fine" to Grandma and mean it. After all, I'd faced plenty of hard things: divorce, coming here alone, packing my life into boxes.

But I wasn't brave enough yet.

"Yes," I said.

Chapter 10

The next day, Cayman didn't show up right away. I ate slowly, because I had it all planned out. In between bites over breakfast, I'd say, "Oh, by the way, the white bird is a gyrfalcon."

I had memorized all the facts to tell him. Cayman would be so surprised. Maybe he'd even spit out his orange juice.

But though I ate very slowly, I finished breakfast without any sign of him.

He didn't come while I was leaving Miss Agatha's food in her fancy new rummage-sale bowl under the hydrangea bush.

Or while I took some photos of Grandma's garden to send to Mom and Dad.

Or while I studied the photo Mom had sent me of my bookcase at home and chose which books to keep.

Or while I helped Grandma wash the dishes.

I actually felt a little disappointed. I wanted to show off a bit, but even more, I was surprised how nice it was to have another kid around sometimes.

"Do you want to take Cayman some muffins?" Grandma asked, getting a basket.

"Okay." I was glad to have an excuse to walk over to his house. I could still tell him about the gyrfalcon, even if it wasn't exactly the way I'd planned.

On the way, I shrugged off my disappointment. It was the kind of perfect day after a storm where the sky looks extra blue, and it was exciting to walk to Cayman's house alone. At home, there were only a few places Mom let me walk by myself. And I had to text her as soon as I got there.

So it was freeing and a little scary to go places alone in Stone Harbor. To push away my nerves, I concentrated on naming the bird sounds I heard. The *caw* of an American crow. The *cheer-cheer-cheer* of a northern cardinal. The *peter-peter-peter* of a tufted titmouse.

But when I got close to Cayman's house, I saw two

cars parked on the side of the road. One had a Maine license plate. The other was from Massachusetts.

Oh, that's why he wasn't at breakfast, I thought. His family had company. I hoped the six muffins I'd brought would be enough.

His mom was outside, holding a mug and leaning against their porch railing. It seemed weird that she'd be by herself if they had company, but I didn't really think about it much.

"Hi," I called. "Is Cayman around?"

She looked up and saw me. "He's down at the Point," she said impatiently. "I don't know what's taking him so long."

"Oh," I said. "Thanks. I brought you some muffins. My grandma made them."

Anger flashed across Cayman's mother's face. "Your grandmother needs to mind her own business!" she said. Then she stomped into the house, letting the screen door slam behind her.

I stood there frozen. I didn't get yelled at like that very often. I wouldn't have been more shocked if she'd slapped me. I could feel tears coming.

Should I leave the muffins on the steps? Cayman's

mom obviously didn't want them, but if I took them home, Grandma would ask why. I was embarrassed to tell her that I'd offended Cayman's mom.

And I couldn't even remember what I'd said.

I decided to throw the muffins into the woods on my walk home. But as I started back down the driveway, another car stopped in front of the others.

This car had a New Hampshire license plate. A woman got out, then grabbed a tripod and a backpack from the back seat.

"Hey there! How do I find the eagles' nest?" she called to me.

"It's at the Point," I said. "There's a path, but you have to cross this yard and—"

"Thanks! I'll go ask permission at the house."

"No! You can't!"

Cayman's mom was already upset. I didn't want to do anything to make her angrier. "The lady who lives there has been sick. She doesn't want to be bothered," I explained.

"I've driven two hours to get here," the woman said, frustration in her voice. "Is there another way to get to the Point?"

"By boat, I guess," I said.

She shook her head. Then she looked across the lawn. "Is that the path over there?"

"Yes, but—"

"I'll be very respectful," she said, starting across the lawn. "I promise."

"Wait!" This woman obviously wouldn't listen to no. I looked back at Cayman's house. The front door was still closed. Hopefully, his mom wouldn't see what was happening.

I wanted to make sure the lady stayed off their lawn. "Let me take you. But hurry, okay?" I led her along the edge of the woods instead of crossing the grass. The sooner we were out of sight of the house, the better.

We were almost at the path when the woman said, "I hear there was a gyrfalcon sighting?"

I stopped walking so suddenly that she ran into me. "Where'd you hear that?" I asked, slowly turning around. I couldn't believe it! Mrs. Wells had promised it would be our secret.

"On the Maine Birding website," the woman said. "The person who posted said Stone Harbor and mentioned a bald eagles' nest. I just asked at the little market where I could find an eagles' nest."

My breath caught in my throat. I looked back across the lawn at the other two cars parked on the road.

And my heart sank.

Mrs. Wells hadn't brought people to see the gyrfalcon.

I had.

Chapter 11

"Step where I step," I said, leading the woman slowly over the rocks at the shore. "The seaweed is slippery."

I wished the woman would hurry up, but she moved carefully to protect her camera and tripod. Swinging my basket of muffins, I could hear voices up ahead, including Cayman's. I really needed to explain everything to him.

When we finally rounded the Point, Cayman was sitting on the rocks next to an older man with a fancy camera. Another man had a camera around his neck, but he was looking through a scope pointed in the direction of the island.

The older man waved to us. "Hey, Kittiwake! Did you get a twitch?"

The woman behind me called back, "Of course,

BirdingBen. A lifer is always worth the drive."

I turned to her. "A lifer?"

She smiled. "A *lifer* is a wild bird that you've seen for the first time in your life. And a *twitch* is when you hear about a rare bird and you just *have* to go see it for yourself."

"When you follow that twitch, you become a twitcher!" BirdingBen said.

The other man held out his hand to shake ours. "Nice to meet you. I'm BlackScoter on the boards."

"Oh, it's great to meet you in real life!" Kittiwake said. "I always enjoy the photos you post."

"Mia, our white bird is a gyrfalcon!" Cayman's eyes shone with excitement. "BirdingBen says gyrfalcons usually live up in the Arctic. So it's rare to find one here—especially in summer."

"Wow," I said, forcing myself to smile. "That's really amazing."

Earlier I'd wanted so badly to one-up Cayman, but now I felt guilty. I'd upset his mom and more people knew about the gyrfalcon.

"The gyrfalcon was in the tree above us when we got here, but Rachel chased her away," Cayman said. "We're waiting to see if she comes back."

"She?" I asked.

BirdingBen nodded. "The gyr is a juvenile female."

My bird was a girl, and I couldn't believe she was just a kid. She'd fought back against the eagles so fiercely!

"She's a vagrant, which means she's outside her normal range," BirdingBen explained. "Maybe she got blown off course in a storm. Or started looking for territory of her own and simply went too far. That's just guessing, though."

Grandma had said the gyrfalcon was a bird of mystery. "Will she know how to get back home?" I asked.

"Her instincts may kick in and send her back north," BirdingBen said.

"What if that doesn't happen?" I asked. "Could she live here?" Maybe Maine could become her home away from home, like it was for me?.

"Possibly. Some vagrants stay and adapt to their new homes," BirdingBen said. "It's one way that birds expand their range. A bird goes somewhere new and succeeds there. Climate change has made that happen faster for some species. Some birds have already moved into new areas where they haven't lived historically."

"But, BirdingBen, you have to admit that's unlikely in

this case," BlackScoter said. "To live here, she'd have to adapt to more than a new environment. A gyr's main diet is ptarmigan, and those birds don't live here."

Kittiwake nodded. "As special as it is to see vagrants, many do end up in a place they can't survive long-term. And even if she did adapt, without another gyrfalcon to mate with, she'd be the only one. It'd be a lonely life for her."

I felt a sharp pang in my heart, thinking of my gyrfalcon alone for her whole life. Most of what made Maine feel like my home away from home was Grandma. Stone Harbor wouldn't feel the same without her.

"Can't someone just catch her and send her home? Like on an airplane or something?" Cayman asked.

BirdingBen shook his head. "There are laws to protect birds, and there's nothing really wrong with her. She's just out of her range. You can't trap a healthy wild gyrfalcon—even the Warden Service wouldn't do that."

"Which is why it's so special that we get to see her," Kittiwake said. "I've seen a few gray morph gyrs, but never a wild white one. It's really like finding buried treasure!"

It seemed weird that something as terrible for the bird as being lost could make people so happy. Looking across to the island, I wondered, *Is the gyrfalcon scared to find herself here, alone and lost? Does she wish she could go home?*

"When I got here, I was surprised the place wasn't already crawling with photographers and birders!" BirdingBen said. "We're lucky we don't have to fight for a good viewing spot."

"Give it a day," BlackScoter said. "Most people probably haven't seen the post yet."

"The minute I saw Merlin11's first photo on Maine Birders, I started packing my camera gear!" Kittiwake said. "I couldn't wait to see the gyr for myself!"

"Someone took a photo?" Cayman asked. "I thought Mia and I were the only people who'd seen it."

"Oh. Um. Hey, my grandma made some strawberry muffins," I said quickly, to change the subject. "Who'd like one?"

"Oooh, strawberry," BlackScoter said as I passed the basket around. "This is a special day, indeed."

"Look!" Kittiwake said excitedly, pointing at the sky. "Here she comes!"

My basket fell onto the rocks as BirdingBen grabbed his camera. "Flight shot!"

The gyrfalcon was soaring across the channel toward

us, as beautiful and magical-looking as ever. Snow-white feathers against the blue sky.

But something big had shifted in me. I imagined she'd come as a hopeful, good luck sign for me, but now I knew she was young and a long way from home and maybe things would never be the same for her.

And I knew exactly how that felt.

I heard a steady stream of shutter clicks as she flew overhead and then landed on a branch.

"Cayman, I know I promised we'd only be here an hour," BirdingBen said. "But would it be okay if we hang out here a while longer? Now that she's back?"

"Oh yes, please!" Kittiwake said. "I've only just arrived!"

Cayman sighed. "I guess so."

He seemed impatient to leave, though, and I felt terrible. I knew Cayman's mom was already wondering what was taking him so long.

And I was worried about the gyrfalcon. Mrs. Wells had said the fewer people who knew the gyrfalcon was here, the better. But BirdingBen had said he was surprised the Point wasn't crawling with photographers and birders.

I had to do something. "I should get home," I said. "I didn't tell Grandma I'd be gone this long."

Cayman nodded. "Tell her thanks for the strawberry muffins."

Walking home with my empty basket, I made a decision. I hadn't meant to bring people here, but maybe I could stop more from coming. BlackScoter had said most people probably hadn't seen the post yet.

I pulled out my phone and opened the message board. I had twenty new responses to my photo. Without even reading them, I clicked the little delete icon on both of my messages.

It wiped everything away—my messages and all the replies.

Good. Now no one else could read about the gyrfalcon. After a few days, interest would die down. Then it'd be like it had never happened.

And then I could figure out how to help the gyrfalcon get home.

Chapter 12

When I got back to Grandma's, I told her that Cayman had liked the muffins and that we'd seen the gyrfalcon. I wanted to tell her the rest, how Cayman's mom had yelled at me and the birders had shown up. But I was embarrassed and wondered if she might be disappointed in me. Or she'd tell Mom and I might lose my phone. Or they'd think I wasn't responsible enough to do things by myself.

"Can I help you with anything?" I asked, wanting to make up for it. "Can I reach something that's up high? Or is there any weeding I can do? Or do you need anything at the store?"

"Oh my goodness," Grandma said. "You're so helpful, Mia. Well, I'm down to my last can of cat food. Would you mind walking down to Holbrook's to get some?"

"Glad to," I said.

Grandma took some money from her purse. "This should be enough for six cans of Seafood Medley. That's her favorite. If that's not available, Miss Agatha will eat Chicken Supreme. Just don't get the beef one. For some reason, she turns her nose up at that one."

"Miss Agatha is pretty fussy for a stray cat," I said, laughing.

Grandma grinned. "Just because she's down on her luck, it's no reason to let go of her standards. There's enough money for you to get some saltwater taffy, too."

Normally, I'd like that. Holbrook's General Store had a whole row of glass jars full of different types of saltwater taffy: blueberry, peppermint, orange, banana, strawberry, peanut butter, root beer, mint, maple, lemon, and watermelon. Each one was individually wrapped in waxy paper. Over the years, I've tried them all, but my favorites were blueberry, strawberry, and watermelon.

Today my stomach felt too mixed up even for those.

Walking to the store, I wondered how something so small as wanting to know something first could have snowballed into something so huge as not telling Grandma the whole truth. I had only meant to keep a little secret for a short time. I didn't mean for that secret to *grow*.

Usually, there were a few cars parked in front of the store along the street, but today cars were parked all the way to the church. Maybe someone in town was hosting a party?

I hoped they weren't all there to buy cat food.

Inside the store, there was a mix of townspeople I recognized and some tourists I didn't. One of Grandma's neighbors waved to me. "Mia, good to see you! Your grandma said you were coming to visit."

"Good to see you, too, Mrs. Eaton," I said, trying to smile. "I'm just getting some cat food for Miss Agatha, Grandma's stray cat."

"Oh, that cat eats my Max's cat food, too!" Mrs. Eaton laughed. "She's probably getting fed all over the neighborhood. Feline freeloader!"

"*Smart* feline freeloader!" I said.

"Tell your grandma I have lots of rhubarb this year if she'd like some," Mrs. Eaton said. "And say hi to Beanie from me. We all miss her here at home."

"I will," I promised. It was funny how the people of Stone Harbor talked about Mom like she belonged there, even though she hadn't lived there for years. They'd saved her place for her, like when one of my friends saved my seat in the school cafeteria. It was my spot, even if I wasn't in it.

Stepping around some people looking at a map, I grabbed a plastic shopping basket and headed toward the pet supplies.

"It's a lifer for me," a voice said.

I stopped walking. A lifer? Kittiwake had said that word earlier.

Only my eyes moved to look at a man buying water at the cash register. I'd never seen him before.

"Well, good luck!" Mr. Holbrook said, ringing him up. "We have many birds here for you to enjoy."

"Oh, but this one's very special," the man said.

He must've seen my post before I deleted it. I quickly put all the cans of Seafood Medley into my shopping basket and then added three Chicken Supremes.

"Hey, can I leave my car here and walk to the Point?" the man asked.

"Not here at the store," Mr. Holbrook said. "It's been a very busy morning, and I need the parking spaces. You can park in the church's lot since it's not Sunday. The path to the Point is on private property, though. You'll have to ask the homeowners for permission. It's a woman and her son."

"Thanks!" the man said. "How do I get there?"

"I'll draw you a map." As Mr. Holbrook drew on the back of the man's receipt, I got into the checkout line behind Mrs. Eaton.

"What's this all about?" Mrs. Eaton asked.

"Oh, haven't you heard?" Mr. Holbrook said. "Some big falcon is harassing the eagles' nest. You might want to keep an eye on Max."

"Dear me!" She turned to the man. "Would it hurt a cat?"

The man shrugged. "It can take a bird the size of a Canada goose. So I'd keep cats inside. It's better for the birds, anyway."

The birders had said the regular food for the gyrfalcon wasn't available here. Would she get desperate?

"But I've heard it's more interested in the eaglets," the man said. "So I'm hoping to get shots of the gyrfalcon and the adult eagles together! That would be a once-in-a-lifetime sort of shot!"

"Did you say something's harassing the eagles' nest?"

I looked over to see Mr. Giffin from the real estate

office. "Are the eaglets okay? What about HW and Rachel?"

"I don't know," Mr. Holbrook said. "I think I'll go check on them tonight after I close up. We don't usually get so many people on a Wednesday morning!"

"I'll go with you!" Mr. Giffin said. "If I didn't have a two o'clock showing, I'd go now. I'm worried about the eaglets. They need to be fed! Rachel and HW can't spend precious hunting time chasing off some intruder bird and a bunch of bird-watchers! We've got to do something!"

Do something? A *bunch* of bird-watchers?

My heart sank as I imagined a long line of cars along the road at Cayman's house.

Outside, I immediately dropped my shopping bag onto a bench and sat down. I knew I'd already spent too much time on my phone, but this was an emergency. I logged into the message board to be sure my message had been deleted.

The first thing I saw was a new message with the subject: "A WHITE GYRFALCON!!!!"

BirdingBen, BlackScoter, and Kittiwake had already posted messages with amazing photos of my gyrfalcon.

Some so close up that I could see the yellow ring around her dark eye.

BlackScoter's message even included a map to Stone Harbor and directions to the path at Cayman's house.

And worst of all, BirdingBen had replied to his post:

Thank you, Merlin11! If you're around today, maybe we can buy you a coffee and a piece of pie at the restaurant? We really appreciate you pointing us to this gorgeous bird and giving us the chance to see her! Message me!

A chill went up my back. Because I hadn't started these posts, I couldn't delete them. I stared at one of the beautiful photos of the gyrfalcon, feeling helpless.

"How do I get to the Point?" a voice asked.

I looked up from my phone. It was a woman holding a camera.

"I don't know," I lied.

Chapter 13

When I got back to Grandma's, Cayman was talking to her near the mailbox. He looked upset. I braced myself in case he was mad at me, but he barely looked in my direction.

"Mom had an appointment and she couldn't even get out of our driveway!" he said angrily. "I had to walk all the way to the Point to find the guy who owned the car and ask him to move it!"

"That's such a shame!" Grandma said.

I swallowed hard. I knew the people I'd seen at the store were also on their way to his house.

"I counted seventeen cars already! Our neighbors are mad that the road gets blocked, and it's stressing Mom out to have all these people knocking on the door, asking to use the path!" Cayman said. "And one woman showed up right when Mom was trying to rest. Mom didn't feel well, and the lady caught her at a bad time. I've never seen my mom that mad. After the woman left, Mom yelled at me, like it was all my fault. And I didn't do *anything*!"

I felt awful that I'd caused all this. I wanted to fix things, but I didn't know how to even start. I hadn't meant to, but I'd set something in motion that was gaining speed all on its own now.

And I couldn't stop it.

"I wish the gyrfalcon would go back where she belongs," Cayman said. "That would be a good first step. Then things would quiet down and maybe get back to normal. I would think the gyrfalcon would *want* to go home."

Suddenly, I missed everything: my parents, my house, my bedroom, and, most of all, knowing where I belonged.

I want to go home, I thought, tears coming to my eyes.

But home wasn't even home anymore. Sometimes there is no going back to normal.

Was that how the gyrfalcon felt, too? Like too much had changed and now there was no way back?

"Maybe she doesn't know how to get home," I said softly.

"Oh, Mouse," Grandma said, putting her arm around me. "Don't fret. Come inside. I'll make us some iced tea and we'll figure something out."

"We need to help her," I said, following Grandma and Cayman into the kitchen. "Mr. Giffin and Mr. Holbrook are worried about the eaglets. Mr. Giffin said they had to *do* something."

"Do what?" Grandma asked, setting a glass of iced tea in front of me.

But my throat felt too tight to drink anything. "I don't know, but I'm worried they'll hurt her," I said.

"Can we try feeding the gyrfalcon?" Cayman asked. "If she wasn't hungry, maybe she'd leave the eaglets alone."

Grandma shook her head. "I'm sure that's illegal, and easy food might encourage her to stay. She has all the instincts she needs to go home, but maybe she just needs some encouragement to go, a little push."

"A push?" I asked.

"I have an idea," Grandma said. "It might not work, though."

"What idea? Tell us!" I said. "Even if it doesn't work, it's still better than *no* idea."

"Last fall I had a hawk hanging around the bird feeder," Grandma said. "I read a suggestion in a gardening magazine to hang some old music CDs in the trees. They're small and shiny. The wind moves them around, and the sunlight reflects off them. It was a simple idea and it didn't harm the hawk at all. But it did encourage him to leave and hunt elsewhere."

I imagined a tree full of shiny circles reflecting in the sun, like a sparkly Christmas tree. Would that really work?

"If it scares away the gyrfalcon, won't it scare the eagles, too?" Cayman asked.

"The eagles have a big reason to stay nearby," Grandma said. "They won't abandon their babies. And if the gyrfalcon is like the hawk, it will go quickly."

"Maybe we could try it for a few hours?" I suggested. "And if it didn't work, we could take the CDs down again."

Cayman didn't look convinced. "I don't know if we can even hang the CDs high enough. I can climb trees, but most of the trees at the Point are pretty skinny at the top."

"I can do it." I had no idea if I really could, but I had

to stop what I'd started. It was my fault and I was willing to try anything to fix it. "It's better than doing nothing, right?"

He shrugged. "I guess so. Okay. Let's try it."

As Grandma went to get the CDs, Cayman and I took our iced tea onto the porch to wait. We startled Miss Agatha out from under the steps.

That was the closest Miss Agatha had ever come to the house. When I first arrived, I didn't like Miss Agatha hanging around because of the songbirds. But seeing her so close to Grandma's house, I felt sorry for her.

"I feel bad for Miss Agatha," Cayman said. "I think she wants to belong here, but she's scared to get too close."

I nodded. "Grandma thinks her owner abandoned her. How could someone do that?"

"Maybe they didn't have a choice," Cayman said. "Some people want to do the right thing, but they just can't."

"Well, if they drove away and left her, then they didn't try hard enough," I said sharply. "She trusted them, and they let her down! She didn't have a choice, but they did."

I heard a little sound, like a puff of air pulled in. I looked over at Cayman and saw tears welling up in his eyes.

He handed me his empty iced-tea glass. "It's not always that simple, Mia."

"I'm sorry," I said. "Did I—"

"I need to go home," he said, blinking fast. "Let's do the CDs tomorrow. It's too late today."

It wasn't late at all. But he was already walking down the driveway. I stared after him, my mouth open. Sometimes I felt like I didn't know him at all.

When Grandma came outside carrying the box of CDs, she asked, "Where's Cayman?"

"I think I hurt his feelings," I said. "We were just talking about Miss Agatha. I said if someone left her, they should've tried harder. He looked like he might cry."

Grandma sighed. "I'm sure it wasn't you."

But I didn't see how that could be true.

Chapter 14

The next morning, I woke to the sound of the foghorn, pulsing like a deep breath. Usually, I loved the fog. It carried a saltwater smell up from the harbor and I liked the way its dampness clung to my skin.

But today I felt as mixed as the weather. The fog would keep the sun from reflecting on the CDs. But a foggy day wouldn't make for good photos, so that might keep the birders away.

The weather report on my phone said it should clear by midmorning. So after breakfast, I headed to Cayman's house, carrying the box of old music CDs, a ball of yarn to help us hang them in the trees, scissors, and Grandma's bicycle helmet.

I had to promise her I'd wear that for tree climbing.

This time, there were no cars parked along the road by Cayman's house. But there were two new handwritten NO PARKING signs nailed to the trees. There were two more signs, one on each side of the path to the Point.

NO TRESPASSING

PRIVATE PROPERTY

Cayman's mom was in the yard. I steeled myself. *Is she still mad at me?* I stayed on the road just in case.

"Cayman!" she yelled.

When he came outside, she said to him, "I thought fresh air would do me good, but I think I'll go inside and rest."

"Good idea." Cayman held out his hand to help her up the steps. "Lock the door, okay? If someone knocks, just ignore it. I won't be gone long."

Then he looked at me. "Let me get her into bed. She's not feeling well. Some sleep will make her feel better, though."

I nodded. "Sure."

I waited long enough that the box got heavy, and I set it on the ground. I wondered if he was coming back. Or maybe I should just go home and come back later.

Finally, the door opened.

When Cayman returned, I thought he'd explain, but he just picked up the box of CDs and the bicycle helmet and started down the path between the PRIVATE PROPERTY and NO TRESPASSING signs.

Something was obviously wrong with his mom. I wanted to know what it was, but it felt too personal and awkward to ask.

"It's supposed to get sunny later. So this is perfect," he said. "We can hang the CDs this morning while it's foggy, and then when it's sunny later, maybe it'll work."

He was talking like nothing had happened. Like everything was normal and I hadn't hurt his feelings yesterday and his mom wasn't sick enough to have to stay inside.

He obviously didn't want to talk about it, though. So I tried a joke to smooth things over. "These CDs will look like we're decorating the trees for Christmas. The neighbors will wonder what's up."

"They already talk about us," Cayman said bitterly. "What's one more thing?"

I was surprised at the anger in his voice. Maybe people talking about you was why Mom always said "too close" when Grandma said she liked how the road kept the town small and the neighbors close.

I'd always loved Stone Harbor. For me, it was the magical place where Grandma lived, full of nature and people who knew me. A place where I felt like I belonged without ever trying.

But Cayman had said coming to visit was different from living here. So for the first time, I tried to imagine it his way. What if I were a new person in a small town where everyone knew everyone else? And what if I had to start a new school with no friends yet?

It didn't take much to imagine how hard that would be. I didn't want to move and change schools, either.

And just because you've moved in doesn't mean you belong.

"Why'd you move here?" I asked, truly wanting to know.

"Mom wanted a change," Cayman said. "But not every change is a good one."

I nodded. "I hate when my mom and dad make a big decision that affects me—like moving—and then they feel bad if I'm not okay with it."

He looked over, interested. "Yeah. I know what you mean."

"At first the divorce was like that for me, too," I said.

"Now I'm glad, because Mom and Dad stopped fighting so much. My parents are happier now, and I like my mom's boyfriend and my dad's wife. But in the middle, it was hard."

"My parents got divorced, too," Cayman said. "I was only five, but I remember it. My dad said he was divorcing Mom but not me. I think he just said that to make himself feel better about leaving, though. He took a new job in Oregon, and I barely ever see him now. Sometimes I wish he'd been meaner."

"Meaner?" I asked, surprised anyone would ever think that.

"It'd give me a reason to forget about him," Cayman said. "But if he just doesn't care, it means I don't matter."

"At least you have your mom," I said, then kicked myself. Maybe that was a hurtful thing for me to say when I got to see both my parents. And it was obvious he was taking care of her sometimes, instead of the other way around. "I'm sure it was hard to move here, though."

"I hoped it would be better here, but it's worse," Cayman said. "Your grandmother is the best part of living here."

When I first came, I was jealous of their friendship. But I was surprised to realize I'd stopped minding so much that I wasn't the only kid in Grandma's life. "She likes you, too," I said. "I can tell."

For the first time, I felt like we were stepping across a line toward becoming real friends, not just kids who did stuff together because they had to or because they just lived near each other.

As we neared the Point, I could barely see the island across the channel. The fog softened all the colors and sharp lines. It looked like a watercolor background, just a hint of what was there.

"The fog is burning off," Cayman said. "I can already feel the air changing."

Like us.

HW was bringing a fish to the nest. "Let's wait until the eaglets are done eating," Cayman said, sitting down on a big rock. "I don't want to risk bothering them now."

"Good idea. We need to tie loops of yarn to the CDs anyway."

"Make the loops big," Cayman said as I unrolled the yarn. "It'll be easier to hang them on the branches. We won't hang the CDs right next to the nest. Just in the surrounding trees."

Always telling me what to do. But it didn't bother me as

much as usual. Maybe he just didn't know how to say things differently.

In between cutting and tying yarn, I looked up at the trees around me. Many of the lowest branches were over my head. Why did I say I could climb them?

"So I have to admit something to you," I said.

"What?"

"I've never climbed a tree," I said.

"Never?" he asked.

"Not even a little one," I said. "But I'm going to do it today, even if it scares me."

"I'll show you my starter tree," Cayman said. "It has some low branches, and then you can cross to another tree from there."

Cross to another tree? That didn't sound safe at all.

As soon as the eaglets were done with their breakfast, I put on the bike helmet. "I promised Grandma I'd wear this."

Cayman smiled. I thought he might make fun of me. But he just picked up half the CDs. "Ready?"

"Yes." I still wasn't sure I could do it. But I strung half the CDs on to my arm so I'd have both hands free for climbing.

Cayman's starter tree was an oak with a large branch that I could reach from the ground. "Follow me. Hold on to the smaller branches to help you climb, but always keep close to the trunk," Cayman said. "Only put your foot on a big, thick branch and test it first, okay? Don't be afraid to change your mind if you're not sure of a branch."

"Okay," I squeaked. I had tried to answer with confidence, but scared won out.

As Cayman climbed onto a second big branch, I pulled myself onto the first. I held on to the same smaller branches that he had. As I stood up, I hugged the tree trunk. My knees felt a little wobbly, but I was off the ground!

In a tree!

"Now step up here. This is a good second climbing branch," he said as he climbed onto a third. "I'm going to leave the lower branches for you to string CDs, okay? Because you haven't done this as much as me."

When I first arrived, I would have been mad at him for pointing out that he was better at tree climbing. But today I knew it was true. Someone had to do the lower branches, and I didn't want to climb as high as he was going.

I didn't dare look down as I climbed. *Just look at this*

branch and the next one, I told myself. *As Grandma says, figure it out as you go.*

On the fourth branch, I hugged the trunk and let myself look outward. A breeze moved the fog over the water. Wispy and graceful, it looked like the air and the water were dancing together.

Above me, Cayman was hanging CDs, the breeze swinging them around.

I couldn't believe I was doing this! Then, from the corner of my eye, I saw a flash of white. Hugging the tree tightly, I turned my body for a better look.

The gyrfalcon had landed a few trees away, in a spruce. Against the green needles, her white feathers stood out sharply. She was close enough that I could see the tiny sharp hook of her beak.

She watched me curiously.

My heart hurt with how beautiful she was. Weird to think beauty can hurt, but it just does sometimes.

Then I saw the people.

Down below, a man and a woman were standing on the rocks. How had they gotten there? Had they ignored the NO TRESPASSING sign and come down the path anyway?

I scowled at them, but they hadn't seen me yet.

They were staring up at the gyrfalcon.

"She's right there!" the man said. "Wow!"

"But she's not in a good spot," the woman complained. "Those branches are in the way."

"Well, I didn't drive this far for nothing." The man took out his phone. Suddenly, a cry sounded, fierce and urgent.

Kak-kak-kak!

The gyrfalcon snapped her gaze away from me to look around.

The man held his phone up high, and the cry sounded again. He was playing a gyrfalcon alarm call on his phone.

My gyrfalcon answered.

Was the call upsetting her? Or was she excited to find another gyrfalcon? Either way, she was reacting to the recorded call as if there were a real bird nearby. I felt terrible that the man was tricking her.

"It's not working," the woman said. "I want it to come closer. Or at least get out from behind those branches."

The man picked up a small rock from the beach. I thought maybe he was going to skip rocks into the ocean, but he was facing the wrong way.

"I'll make it fly," he said.

"Give me a minute," the woman said. "I want to change lenses."

The man threw the rock, hitting a branch a few trees away from the gyrfalcon.

What was he doing? He might've hit her!

"I told you to give me a minute!" the woman said. "I wasn't ready!"

"It didn't fly anyway," the man said, irritated.

The gyrfalcon looked stressed. She paced on the branch and then screeched. Was she trying to call to the bird she'd heard?

The man picked up another rock.

"Wait!" I yelled.

The couple startled. "What was that?" the man said. "Did you hear someone?"

The woman peered up through the trees, and then our eyes met. I glared at her. "Oh. It's just a kid," she told the man.

"It's *two* kids!" Cayman yelled above me. "And you're not allowed here! It says no trespassing."

"Don't you dare throw rocks!" I called out. "You might hurt her!"

"I'm not going to *hit* it," the man said. "Just make it fly so my wife can get a good photo."

Before I could yell again, he threw the second rock. It hit another branch, swishing through the spruce needles near the gyrfalcon.

It was too close. The gyrfalcon lifted her wings.

"Get the flight shot!" the man cried as the gyrfalcon leaped off the branch into the air. "Get it! There she goes!"

"I'm not ready!" the woman screamed at him.

As the gyrfalcon flew out over the water toward the island, I felt a huge sigh of relief. *Ha!* She had escaped them. She landed at the top of a tree on the island. No one could throw a rock that far.

The man kicked a clump of seaweed. "I can't believe I drove all this way and you didn't get the shot!"

"I told you! I wasn't ready!" the woman snapped at the man. "Why didn't you wait before you threw it?"

"Watch out, Mia!" Cayman was climbing down so quickly that I could only get out of his way. I hugged the trunk to let him pass.

"You need to get out of here!" Cayman shouted at the couple. "This is my mom's property, and you're trespassing."

"If you don't leave, I'll call the police!" I added.

The woman looked at us. "It's a terrible day for photos, anyway," she said bitterly. "The sky is all white."

As they turned and made their way over the rocks, my knees trembled with relief. Then I heard the man say, "The weather is improving, though. On the drive here, I saw a place to rent kayaks and boats. That island isn't very far."

The man turned back to Cayman and me with a mean smile. "No one owns the water."

And I knew something bad was about to happen.

Chapter 15

As the fog burned off, the gyrfalcon's white body stood out sharply against the dark trees at the far end of the island. She looked alone and exposed, in a place she didn't belong.

Cayman and I stayed at the Point to be sure the couple didn't sneak back up the path. We stayed so long that my stomach was growling for lunch and we had hung almost every CD.

"Do you think that couple gave up?" I asked.

"I hope so," he said. "I should get home and check on my mom."

"I'll keep watch," I said. "And I'll come get you if anything happens."

He nodded. "Okay."

The sun on my face felt nice. So I closed my eyes and listened to the waves swishing as they hit the rocks. It reminded me of sizzling, like the sound of Grandma making pancakes.

That thought made me even hungrier.

Off in the distance, I heard a motor. It didn't sound like a lobster boat, though. As the sound got louder, I opened my eyes.

It was a speedboat. Even without binoculars I recognized the man driving the boat and the woman beside him.

Cayman was almost at the path. "They're back!" I called to him.

He turned to look. The boat had stopped in the water near the island. The woman stood up in the boat and pointed her camera at the trees.

Even from our side of the channel, I could see the gyrfalcon's white body at the top of the tallest island tree.

"Well, at least they should have a good view from there," Cayman called back to me. "Maybe they'll leave if they get some photos."

I nodded, though inside, I was still worried. The gyrfalcon looked vulnerable all alone at the top of the tree.

Please just take your photos and leave her in peace, I wished. *You have a good view of her now.*

But deep inside me, I knew it wouldn't be enough. The woman wanted a flying shot, and the man was willing to do anything to get it.

And this time I was too far away to stop him.

Sure enough, the man picked up something from the boat. He pulled back his arm like he was about to throw it.

"Don't!" I screamed as loudly as I could.

The man startled at my voice, and it ruined his aim. A rock flew right toward the tree where the gyrfalcon was perched.

She lifted her wings to fly, but the rock struck her hard.

I watched a blaze of white falling through the tree branches. Down, down, down she bounced from branch to branch.

Then I didn't see her at all.

Cayman and I both ran to the edge of the water. But there was nothing we could do, with the channel between us and the island.

"Look what you made me do!" the man shouted across the channel to me. "You stupid kids! If you hadn't yelled, I wouldn't have hit it!"

"*You* threw the rock!" Cayman shouted back.

The man started the boat.

"Wait! You can't just leave her there!" I cried. "You have to see if she's hurt!"

He didn't listen, though.

As the couple's boat roared away, I scanned the island's trees, hoping the gyrfalcon had simply lost her balance, the way she had when Rachel struck her while flying the first day. Maybe she'd fallen but had recovered and was already perched on another branch?

But there was no patch of white anywhere.

"Maybe she's just stunned," I said softly.

"Maybe," Cayman said.

How long had it taken the goldfinch to recover after it hit Grandma's window? I wanted so badly to see the gyrfalcon rise up and fly to the top of the trees again.

But as the minutes passed, I realized it wouldn't be that easy. I had a horrible feeling in my stomach that she was really hurt.

I took out my phone. Even Mom would agree this was an emergency. I wasn't sure how to get help, but I figured Mrs. Wells was a good start. She might not know what to do, but she'd know who to contact.

She answered right away. "Stone Harbor Library. How can I help you?"

"Mrs. Wells, this is Mia. I'm at the Point with Cayman. The gyrfalcon was in a tree on the island." I knew I was talking too fast, but I couldn't help myself. "Some people in a boat threw a rock at her, trying to make her fly. But they hit her!"

Mrs. Wells gasped. "Oh no!"

"She fell and I think she's hurt."

Or dead. But I couldn't bring myself to say it.

"I'll call the Maine Warden Service," Mrs. Wells said. "They'll send someone. Don't worry. I'll call you back when I know the details, okay?"

"Okay." I felt a huge surge of relief, knowing that help was coming and it wasn't all on my shoulders anymore.

"A game warden will check on her," I told Cayman. "Mrs. Wells will call back as soon as she knows more."

"I really have to get home," Cayman said. "I told my mom I wouldn't be gone long—and it's been hours. She'll be mad at me."

"I should go home, too," I said.

We'd only gotten halfway down the path when Mrs. Wells called. "Warden Cooper will be there at two o'clock with his boat. He'll go to the island and check her out," she said. "I asked Mrs. Holbrook if she'd cover for me at the library so I can go, too. Could you and Cayman meet us at the town boat launch and show us exactly where you last saw the gyrfalcon?"

"Yes," I said. "Thank you, Mrs. Wells. I really appreciate your help."

"I'm glad a warden is coming," Cayman said when I told him the plan. "Because I feel like it's my fault she got hurt."

"Your fault?" I was so surprised that I stopped walking and looked at him.

"I shouldn't have shown anyone the way to the Point," Cayman said sadly. "I thought it was cool that we'd found something other people wanted to see. But I should have said no."

"There's no way it's your fault." I couldn't let him think that. "Because it's mine."

He looked at me. "What do you mean?"

I turned away from him, embarrassed. "Before I tell you, I just want to say that if I'd known this would happen, I wouldn't have done it. You have to believe me about that."

"Done what?"

I took a deep breath. "I posted my best photo of the gyrfalcon on a birding message board. I just wanted to find out what kind of bird it was before you did. But then people weren't sure and asked for a better photo. So I tried using the binoculars."

I snuck a look at him. He was staring at me with his mouth open.

Having started this, I had to finish. "Someone asked where the bird was. I didn't think I was really telling them. But I said the town name and mentioned an eagles' nest. They figured out the rest."

"Why'd it even matter who found out first?" Cayman asked, his voice sounding hollow, like it didn't belong to him.

"Well, didn't it matter to *you*?" I asked. "It seems like you always want to be first and best at everything."

"Not if it hurts someone else," he said flatly.

I felt my face getting hot. "I wanted to spend time with Grandma and you were always there. Sometimes it even seemed like you knew more about her than I did! I have to share my parents, but I've never had to share *her* before. I wanted something that was mine."

"It's *all* yours!" he said bitterly. "Don't you see that? And now you've made a mess of my whole life!"

"What? Just because some birders showed up?" I asked. "That's not your whole life!"

"One of those birders told my mom to get help! My mom was having a bad day and she should have been resting! But instead of just saying I'm sorry and leaving her alone, the woman said she should get help! And she started giving her advice and her card and telling her what to do! My mom slammed the door on her and cried all night about it!"

"What kind of help?" I asked.

"That's all you can say?" Cayman snapped. "I'm telling you that it upset my mom and you just want nosy details? Why? So you can blame her, too? You don't understand *anything*!" He started running away from me up the path.

"Wait!" I said.

But he didn't even turn to look at me. Over his shoulder, he said, "I thought we were friends, but we aren't!"

Alone on the path, I felt sick to my stomach. I'd ruined so many things I cared about. The gyrfalcon had been injured and maybe even killed. I'd lied to Grandma. I'd hurt Cayman and wrecked our friendship.

I didn't know how to make any of it right again.

And maybe I'd broken things that couldn't be fixed.

Chapter 16

I didn't know what to do with myself. I knew Grandma would take one look at my worried face and ask questions. So I called her and pretended everything was okay. I told her I was still busy helping the gyrfalcon and I would be home before suppertime. Then I walked to the boat launch and sat at one of the picnic tables to wait. I listened to the waves. I watched boats that came by. I used my finger to trace the names people had carved into the wooden bench.

I tried not to think. It hurt to think about Cayman and the gyrfalcon. So I identified every bird that called.

Teakettle-teakettle-teakettle: Carolina wren.

Kree-aaa: black-backed gull.

Chicka-dee-dee-dee-dee: chickadee.

Finally, just past two o'clock, Mrs. Wells pulled into the boat launch parking lot, followed by a pickup truck towing a small motorboat.

I looked up the road, hoping I'd see Cayman coming, but the road was empty. It was possible that Cayman's mom needed him, but I had a sinking feeling that he didn't come because of me.

"Hi, Mia, this is Warden Cooper," Mrs. Wells said, gesturing to the man in the green uniform.

He smiled at me. "Hi. So I hear we have a famous bird visitor that needs some help?"

I'd never met a game warden, but I'd seen them on TV. I knew one of their jobs was to help wildlife in trouble, and I was glad Mrs. Wells had known who to call.

I tried to smile back, but I was too worried to even fake it. "Hi," I said. "Will you be able to help the gyrfalcon?"

"That depends on what we find," he said. "But we'll do our best for her." The warden took a toolbox, a big fishing net with a long pole, a blanket, heavy leather gloves, and a large dog carrier from his truck. "You two did the right thing by calling."

"I wish we knew the names of the couple that hit her with a rock!" Mrs. Wells said angrily. "I'd like to have them arrested."

The warden nodded. "Yes, I'd like to have a stern word with them! Most birders and photographers are very respectful and careful not to disturb the birds they are photographing. They don't get too close. Or chase the bird. Or do something to change the bird's behavior," he said. "But some people don't put the birds' needs first. They care more about getting a good photo to post online. So it becomes more about showing off for other people than enjoying the bird."

I swallowed hard. It was like he knew what I'd done. I hadn't chased the gyrfalcon or thrown any rocks, but I had gotten caught up in the excitement of seeing people react to the photos I'd taken. And I didn't think about what was the best thing for the gyrfalcon. Showing off to Cayman had been too important to me.

"If a raptor can't hunt, it'll starve. And if it can't rest, it'll become exhausted. Some birds of prey can be literally loved to death by too much attention," he said.

I thought about that as Warden Cooper backed the Jeep and the boat trailer down the ramp next to the wharf.

It was wonderful for us to see something so special as the gyrfalcon, but it hadn't been so wonderful for her. She'd been chased and tricked and hurt. Warden Cooper's words, *Some birds of prey can be literally loved to death*, played over and over in my mind.

I didn't want that for her. I would do anything to change it. But the best possibility was that she had come close to being "loved" to death, and the worst possibility was it had already happened.

Mrs. Wells tied the boat to the wharf and waited while Warden Cooper parked the Jeep.

"Okay, let's go find her," Warden Cooper said, handing me a life preserver. "But when we get to the island, you have to stay in the boat, Mia. A wounded gyrfalcon can still do some serious damage with those talons."

I tried not to let my disappointment show. Even though the talons sounded scary—even scarier than climbing a tree—I wanted to help her. I could tell Warden Cooper didn't want me in the way, though. "I will. I promise."

Before I climbed into the boat, I looked back, just in case Cayman was running toward us to catch up. But no one was in the parking lot.

I sighed. I had told him the time and the place. He wasn't coming.

"Point the way," Warden Cooper said.

Stepping over some oars in the bottom of the boat, I found a spot to sit next to a big first-aid kit. "See those tall trees right at this end of the island? That's the last place we saw her."

"Great," Warden Cooper said. "Hang on tight!"

He wasn't kidding! Warden Cooper drove so fast, the boat bounced on the waves.

My hands hurt from gripping the side of the boat. Grandma had taken me on boat rides on the ocean before, but we'd always been on a bigger, slower tourist boat. Even then, I'd been a little afraid. The spray off the side was always painfully cold and it was so dark below the surface. Who knew what might be down there?

But today, I pushed those worries away. I was more concerned about the gyrfalcon, and the faster we got to the island, the better.

I wondered what we'd find. Would she be hopping around with a broken wing? Or sitting still, panting with her beak open?

Or worst of all, would she be lying in a lifeless heap

at the bottom of the tree? She might never get to go home. And my heart broke for her because I knew that feeling.

Sometimes there's no going backward. Even if our house didn't sell and Mom repainted all the walls the colors they used to be and put everything back where it belonged, it wouldn't be the same.

No matter what, things would be different now—for the gyrfalcon and for me.

At the island, Warden Cooper jumped into the shallow water and tied the boat to a tree. "Mrs. Wells, can you bring the carrier? I'll bring the rest."

Warden Cooper grabbed the big net, huge gloves, blanket, and toolbox. I watched him climb up the sandy bank with Mrs. Wells.

Together they stepped carefully, sweeping brush and tall grasses aside. "I think it was farther back!" I called. "Do you want me to show you?"

"No thanks," Warden Cooper said. "We'll find her. The island's not that big."

I felt so useless staying behind. I moved all around the boat, trying to see from every angle.

Adrenaline rushed through me, but I had nothing to

do and it had nowhere to go. I pulled my feet up onto the boat seat and rested my arms on my knees. *Where are they? What's happening?*

I listened hard for any sounds. Rustling leaves. Snapping twigs. Anything to tell me where Warden Cooper and Mrs. Wells were. Quiet didn't seem like a good sign. Quiet might mean the gyrfalcon was badly hurt or even—

"Oh! There she is!" I finally heard Mrs. Wells say. I let go a deep breath of relief. They'd found her. "She's alive, Mia!" Mrs. Wells yelled. "But she's got her talons tangled in some old lobster rope."

She was alive!

"She must've thrashed around after she fell," I heard Warden Cooper say. "I'll hold her and you cut her free."

Then I heard what sounded like a struggle. I got up and stood on the seat of the boat.

"Mia, I know what I said before," Warden Cooper said. "But we need another set of hands. Can you come here?"

I was out of the boat so fast I almost tipped it over.

My sneakers got wet from jumping in the water, but

I didn't care. I rushed up the bank in the direction I'd seen Warden Cooper and Mrs. Wells go.

Just beyond the first trees, I saw them. The gyrfalcon was upright. Warden Cooper was behind her, holding her wings against her sides.

She looked furious and ready to fight us all.

Relief hit me so hard it made my knees weak. She was alert! She was sitting up! She was mad!

Those had to be good signs.

Mrs. Wells was holding some pruners, but the gyrfalcon was not cooperating. "I'm sorry. She's really stuck. I just can't get close enough to cut the rope away."

"Mia, I want you to take that blanket and throw it over her, except for her feet," Warden Cooper said. "She'll be more relaxed if she can't see. Don't get too close, though. She's feisty."

I shook out the blanket to make it as big as possible. Then I held two corners and walked closer. My hands were shaking. *What if I mess this up? What if I miss?*

I took another step closer.

"Throw it from there," Warden Cooper said. "And then immediately take five big steps backward."

The gyrfalcon was looking at me.

I promise it's not to hurt you, I told her in my mind. *Don't be afraid.*

I threw the blanket wide, like I was spreading it out for a picnic. It covered the gyrfalcon and some of Mrs. Wells, too.

Quickly, I took five steps backward.

Then everything happened fast. Mrs. Wells appeared from under the blanket. She grinned, holding up a snarl of rope in her hand. "Got it!"

Warden Cooper rushed the gyrfalcon into the carrier, blanket and all. Then he pulled out the blanket, like a magician whipping a cloth away. "Whew! We got her!" he said, latching the carrier. "Thanks for your help!"

I was so relieved, but only until I saw the gyrfalcon looking out of the wire door of the carrier. Her eyes looked flat, like the fight had left them.

"Here's your chance for a great photo," Mrs. Wells said to me. "You might never be closer to a wild gyrfalcon than this."

"I don't want to remember her like this," I said. "She doesn't even look like herself."

"She's in pain," Warden Cooper said. "But you can feel proud that you helped her."

"No." I looked down at my soaking sneakers. "I'm not proud at all."

"Why?" I heard Warden Cooper ask. "You were a big help, Mia."

I couldn't look at him. "It's my fault she got hurt," I said softly. "I posted her photo on a birding message board. I wanted to find out what kind of bird it was before my friend did. People on the message board got excited, and someone asked where I'd taken the photo. I didn't think I was really telling him, but I did. It all just exploded into problems."

"Don't be too hard on yourself. You *should* get excited about special things," Warden Cooper said. "I became a game warden because I love spending time outdoors in nature and I want to share that with other people. There's nothing wrong with that. And this gyrfalcon is a rare and beautiful discovery, Mia. You just have to remember that rare, beautiful things are also fragile and need us to protect them."

I glanced at the carrier and into the gyrfalcon's eyes. "At first the attention was exciting for me, but it was never good for *her*."

"Sometimes we do hurt someone else," Warden Cooper said. "But here's something I've learned in life, Mia. You can't always undo that hurt. And not everything can be fixed. But there are always two things you *can* do."

"What are they?" I asked.

"The first is that you can try to make it right," he said. "You're already doing that by helping her."

"What's the second thing?"

"You can learn from it," he said. "Would you do things differently if it happened again?"

I nodded hard. "Definitely."

It was good advice. I knew I had quite a few things to try to make right. Some minor ones like breaking my phone rules and some big ones like ruining my friendship with Cayman and lying to Grandma.

"What'll happen to the gyrfalcon now?" Mrs. Wells asked.

"We're lucky to have a great wild bird hospital in Maine," Warden Cooper said. "I called them before I came and let them know the situation. I'll take her there myself. The head of the hospital said it's the first gyrfalcon patient they've ever had! They're excited to see her, and if anyone can help her, they can."

"Do you think she'll ever get home to the Arctic?" I asked.

Warden Cooper shrugged. "Hard to say. Part of it's up to us, and the rest is up to her. We'll do our part and wait to see if she'll do hers."

The gyrfalcon stared back at me. The more I looked at her, the more I could see that there was a spark of that fierceness still there. Just a flicker, but it gave me hope.

Try to be brave, I told her in my mind. *You already know how. I've seen you take on bald eagles.*

Part of me wished the boat ride would last forever. I knew I might never see the gyrfalcon again, and it was hard to say goodbye.

But the rest of me knew we both had somewhere we needed to go.

In the parking lot, Warden Cooper gave me his business card. "If you want an update on her, just text or send me an email. I can check on her for you."

"Do you want a ride, Mia?" Mrs. Wells asked. "I can drop you at your grandmother's on my way."

"Thank you both," I said. "But I have something to do, Mrs. Wells. Can I borrow a pen?"

"Sure," she said.

On the walk home, I stopped at Cayman's house and left a message on his NO PARKING sign.

It read simply,

The gyrfalcon is safe now.

And I'm really, truly sorry. —Mia

Chapter 17

As soon as I got home, I told Grandma everything. I didn't leave out one detail. "I'm really sorry I didn't tell you earlier," I said. "I was embarrassed and I didn't want you or Mom to be disappointed in me."

"I am disappointed that you didn't trust me to understand," Grandma said. "Mouse, you never needed to compete with Cayman. You're mine and I'm yours—always."

I leaned against her, and she stroked my hair, like she did when I was little. "It seems like the people I love most keep splitting themselves into more pieces," I said. "And my piece gets smaller. I thought it was happening with you, too."

"Never," she said. "Cayman and I are friends, but that

doesn't take anything away from how I feel about you. Love isn't like pizza where a bigger piece for one person means a smaller piece for someone else."

"Or Strawberry Grunt?" I tried to smile. It took some faith to believe that, but maybe I could just trust that Grandma was right. There was enough love to go around, even if I had to share it.

She smiled, too. "Exactly. Did you explain all this to Cayman?"

I shrugged one shoulder. "I tried, but he said I didn't have any reason to be jealous because it's *all* mine." It hurt to remember what he'd said, but I was determined to tell her everything. I hoped she could help me understand and fix things. "I don't know what he meant by that."

"I suspect he feels a bit jealous of *you*," Grandma said. "Cayman's mom has some things that she's working on. I'm sure that's hard for him."

"What kind of things?" I asked.

"He doesn't talk about it, so all I know is town gossip," Grandma said. "But some kids cope with a lot, Mia."

When Cayman first said his mom was sick, I thought he meant something like the flu. But I could see now that it was more than that.

"His mom got mad at me over those strawberry muffins," I said.

Grandma's eyebrows went up. "Why? What did she say?"

I didn't want to tell her, but Grandma said, "No more secrets, Mouse. I need to know."

She was right. *No more secrets*, I promised myself. "Cayman's mom said, 'Your grandmother needs to mind her own business,' and then she slammed the door in my face."

Grandma paused for a long moment. "Oh dear. I thought I was helping. I *meant* it to be a good thing, but she obviously didn't see it that way," she said. "I'm sure it's hard for her, taking care of Cayman all on her own. I've often wondered about Cayman's father. I've never asked, though. I always thought Cayman would tell me if he wanted to."

"He told me a little about his dad," I said. "Cayman doesn't get to see him, but he came from an island called Cayman. That's where his name comes from."

Grandma's eyebrows went up. "Wow. He must have trusted you to have told you, Mia."

I knew she was right. And that hurt.

"At first I just sent him home with some food to help

out," Grandma said, "but then we became real friends. He was lonely, and I was, too. It was nice to have a young person around. It made me miss you less."

I hugged her tight. Grandma knew everyone in Stone Harbor. It never occurred to me that she could ever feel lonely.

"Cayman wouldn't want us to feel sorry for him, though," Grandma said. "That's not what he really needs. He needs friends."

"But what if he doesn't want to be *my* friend now?" I could still hear his words ringing in my ears. "He said we weren't friends."

"Then you'll have to accept no as his answer," Grandma said. "But I do have an idea."

"What?" I asked quickly.

"Cayman is proud, and proud people often find it easier to give help than to take it," Grandma said. "And we will need some help."

"We will?" I asked.

Grandma nodded. "Hearing about the gyrfalcon makes me realize something. You said when you first saw the gyrfalcon, you did what was good for *you,* not what was right for her."

I nodded.

"I'm afraid I've done the same thing with Miss Agatha," Grandma said.

I tilted my head to look at her. It almost felt like she was sharing a secret with me. "What do you mean?" I asked.

"I've grown fond of her," Grandma said. "But this is not where she truly belongs. She needs a real home."

"But you tried," I said. "You put up signs and no one called about her."

Grandma nodded. "Though as the weeks went by, I was glad that no one called. Miss Agatha has felt like mine, even if she wasn't. And I was afraid to find out for certain. So I didn't do anything else to try."

"Like what?" I asked.

"Some pets have a microchip," Grandma said. "It has an owner's information on it. I knew that the Humane Society could scan Miss Agatha to find out if she had one. But I told myself it would be too hard to catch her and she wasn't my cat. Those were excuses. Really, I didn't want to know. You've made me brave enough to find out, Mouse."

"Me?" I couldn't believe she said that. I never thought of myself as brave.

She nodded. "Yes, you. It takes courage to face hard things and to admit when you've made mistakes. You've inspired me."

I gave her a big hug. I still found it hard to believe I was brave, but I also knew deep inside me that she was right that I had faced some hard things. And even though I'd been scared, I'd done it anyway.

"It's easier if you don't have to face those hard things alone," I said. "I'll help you with Miss Agatha. But what'll happen if they don't find a microchip?"

"Then they'll find her a new home," Grandma said. "Either way, she'll be safe. She'll be where a cat is meant to be."

I nodded, but I was pretty sure if they didn't find a microchip, Miss Agatha would be coming right back here to live with Grandma.

"Catching Miss Agatha is going to be a challenge," Grandma said. "I'll call the Humane Society to see if they can loan us some traps." Then she winked at me. "Do you think we might need Cayman's help catching her?"

I smiled. Now I understood her plan. "I'll go over and ask him first thing tomorrow," I said. When I first came, I would've wanted Grandma—and Miss Agatha—to myself, but now I really wanted Cayman to be there.

I didn't know if he'd forgive me, but I wanted to try again to put things right.

And there were two more things I also needed to put right. That night, I posted on the message board.

The gyrfalcon got hurt and has gone to a bird hospital. Someone threw a rock at her trying to make her fly. She isn't here anymore and the path to the Point is marked No Trespassing. So please don't come. And be careful not to disturb the birds you're photographing.

I'd leave the message up for a few days to be sure everyone saw it, then I'd delete my profile.

Texting Mom was harder.

Hi, Mom, I need to tell you something. I broke some phone rules. I went over my time limit a few times, but worse than that, I didn't talk to you about something I wanted to post online. Even though I knew it was something you'd want me to check with you about.

At first, I just wanted a quick answer to a question, but then I let it go on. I created a problem for a friend, lied to Grandma, and a beautiful bird was hurt.

I have learned some big lessons, and I promise I'll

do things differently now. I've told Grandma the truth. The bird is at a bird hospital. I don't know if my friendship can be fixed, though.

I'm sorry, Mom. I promise I'll follow the phone rules from here on. I understand the reasons for them. In fact, I even have a few new phone rules of my own.

Never let the phone become more important than people or animals.

When something is online, it can feel like it doesn't count, but it really does.

I ended the text, **I love you.**

Mom might be mad at me. She might even take my phone away for a while. But I still felt better having done the right thing and told her the truth.

As Grandma always said, the last step of any job is cleaning up.

And that's true, even for mistakes.

Chapter 18

Mom called me immediately. I could hear the disappointment in her voice that I hadn't always told the truth and had broken my phone rules. "I trusted you," she said softly.

Those words felt like they weighed a million pounds each.

"I know. I'm really sorry," I said.

Mom said she'd give me another chance with the phone, but if I broke the rules again, I'd lose my phone for at least a week.

"I'll do better," I promised.

"I know you will," Mom said.

The sure way she said it made me feel better, like she still had faith in me. I told her all about Grandma, Miss

Agatha, Cayman, and the gyrfalcon. Mom told me about the weather and what was happening in town. She kept her promise not to bring up the move unless I asked.

And I couldn't bring myself to ask.

At the end of the call, she said, "Everyone makes some bad decisions, Sweet Pea. I'm proud of you for trying to make things right."

"Thanks," I said. "I love you, Mom."

"I love you more," she said.

I knew I would try my hardest not to let her down again. I didn't know if Cayman would be so forgiving, though.

The next morning, as I walked to his house, my heart beat so hard that it hurt. Usually, I didn't think about walking—I just did it. But on that trip, I had to push myself through every step—like walking through knee-deep water.

And every thought was a scary one.

Cayman might yell at me.

Or slam the door in my face.

Or worse, refuse to even answer the door.

Those thoughts made me want to run away. So I comforted myself by identifying the birdcalls I heard. Blue

jay's screech. Crow's *caw*. Mourning dove's *hoo-hoo-hoo*.
Chickadee's danger call, *chicka-dee-dee-dee*.

If I were a chickadee, I'd do a million *dee*s today.

At Cayman's, no one was in the yard. The PRIVATE
PROPERTY and NO TRESPASSING signs were still up, and my
note was still on the NO PARKING sign.

Maybe he hadn't even seen it.

I took a deep breath as I climbed the porch steps.
Cayman probably can't get madder than he already is, right?
My hand shook as I knocked.

His mom opened the front door. Through the screen
door, I could see she was still wearing pajamas.

"I'm very sorry to bother you," I said. "But I was hoping to talk to Cayman. It'll just take a minute."

"Cayman!" she yelled.

He came to the doorway, but he didn't step out of the
house. He looked irritated, like I was annoying him.
"What do you want?"

"I want to apologize. I screwed up, and I'm really
sorry." I gave him a few seconds, but he didn't say "It's
okay" or even "I never want to see you again."

He just crossed his arms.

"Um. I was wondering if you'd want to come over.

Grandma called the Humane Society. A lady is bringing a couple traps later on today so we can try to catch Miss Agatha to scan her for a microchip. We need hel—"

I couldn't say it. I wanted him to come, but it wasn't right to trick him into it. "It won't feel right without you there," I said instead. "And I miss being friends."

"We were never friends," Cayman said flatly.

It hurt more than anything else he could've said. I'd told him things I hadn't admitted to anyone else, not even to my friends at home that I'd known for years.

"Friends don't lie to you," he said. "You never had any reason to be jealous. You have everything, and you don't even appreciate it."

He closed the door, leaving me standing there alone.

Chapter 19

Cayman didn't come over. After he closed the door on me, I didn't expect him. But Grandma held out hope that he'd show up.

Nancy from the Humane Society brought two wire Havahart traps to try to catch Miss Agatha. "It's good that you called. Living outside might be okay for a cat in the summer, but not when it gets cold."

We set up one of the traps near the hydrangea bush and the other in the tall grass at the edge of the woods.

"The more traps, the more chances we have to catch her," Nancy said. "For each trap, we'll prop one of the doors open. We want her to get used to going in and out of the traps for food."

Nancy put a blob of Seafood Medley on a dish just

inside the opening of each trap. She said that every day we'd move the food farther inside. When the dish of food was all the way in the back of the trap, we'd catch Miss Agatha.

Then Nancy stood a full water bottle upright in the doorway of each trap. "This will hold the door open." The water bottle had a long string tied around the middle. Nancy laid the string along the ground away from the trap as far as it would reach.

"What's the string for?" I asked.

"It allows *you* to decide when it's safe for the door to close," Nancy said. "On the day she goes all the way inside the trap, you'll yank the string. It'll pull the bottle away and the door will close."

Me?

"But what if I pull the string at the wrong time?" I asked.

"She may not try again," Nancy said. "So don't do it until you're sure."

My heart sank. If we didn't catch Miss Agatha, I didn't want it to be my fault. This was so hard. "Can't we just let the trap close on its own?"

"You're apt to catch something else then," Nancy said.

"And if Miss Agatha sees another animal get trapped, she'll learn from that. She's a smart cat, and smart cats are harder to catch!"

Grandma put her arm around me. "We'll try our best. It's all we can do. Right?"

"I guess so." It still felt scary, but I also knew that I could do hard things, especially if I didn't have to do them alone.

Then Nancy set up Grandma's lawn chairs, one at the end of each piece of string. "The chairs are for you to hide behind on the day you catch her. In the meantime, we want her to get used to seeing them here."

"Won't she see our legs under the chair?" I asked.

"Yes, but I still think it'll work," Nancy said. "By that time she should be pretty comfortable with the traps."

I wanted something surer than "I think," but Nancy was busy covering each trap with a big towel, except for the open door. "I'm making it look like a safe hideaway," she said. I didn't like that we were trying to trick Miss Agatha.

It's for a good reason, I told myself. *Just like the gyrfalcon.*

But I knew Miss Agatha probably wouldn't understand that. To her, it would be only scary.

"If she has a microchip, we'll contact her family and get her home," Nancy said. "First step is to catch her, though. Easy enough?"

No. Not at all.

But every day I did what Nancy had told me. I made sure the water bottles stayed in place, propping open the trap doors. I put a little Seafood Medley on dishes and slid them into the traps, a little farther each day.

Grandma and I did puzzles, played board games, went for walks, baked cookies—all things I usually liked, but my heart wasn't always in it.

Cayman still didn't come over. Grandma had said I might have to take no as his answer. Each day that went by, it seemed pretty clear that was his decision.

Until the day Miss Agatha's dishes were all the way at the back of the two traps.

"Today's the day!" Grandma said. "Go make sure everything is set up. I'll be with you in a few minutes. I just have to make a quick phone call first."

"Okay," I said.

I made sure the food was as far inside the traps as possible, the water bottles were holding the doors open, and the strings could be reached easily behind each lawn chair.

It all seemed ready. But as I turned to go get Grandma, I caught a glimpse of movement in the corner of my eye.

Miss Agatha was at the edge of the woods.

Oh no! Not yet! I wasn't behind my lawn chair, and even if I managed to run over there, I could only handle one trap. What if she went in the other one?

And if I left to get Grandma, Miss Agatha might eat the food while I was gone. Then she wouldn't be hungry enough to try again today. She had to be hungry for this to work at all.

No solutions were perfect. So I pulled the food out of both traps to keep her from eating it too early. Then I raced for the house, holding the bowls of cat food.

"Grandma! Come quick!" I called.

But as I turned the corner of the house, my heart jumped.

Cayman was in the driveway.

Chapter 20

Cayman's lips were pressed together as he looked past me to Grandma on the porch.

"What is it, Mia?" she asked me. "I heard you yell."

"Miss Agatha is out back," I said. "Before I ran to tell you, I grabbed the food so she wouldn't eat it while I was gone."

"Oh, good thinking! Cayman's here to help," Grandma said. "I don't know what Nancy was thinking! If I tried to sit on the ground with my knee, you'd have to call the fire department to come help me up again."

I looked from Grandma to Cayman. And suddenly I understood. The phone call she'd made was to Cayman asking him to help.

He wouldn't come for me, but he would for her.

"Hurry and tell Cayman what to do!" Grandma said. "Miss Agatha won't wait around without food."

I knew what she was up to, hoping Cayman and I would work it out if she left us alone together. But that didn't make it easy.

I explained about the traps and what Nancy had told us to do. "And we have to wait until Miss Agatha's totally inside the trap and eating. Nancy said if we don't get it right, we might not get another chance."

"Surely, a second chance is always *possible*," Grandma said.

I knew she wasn't really talking about Miss Agatha then. She was talking about me and Cayman. "I hope so," I said. Because I did.

Cayman didn't say anything, though. He just started around the corner of the house without me.

"I don't think a second chance will happen," I said softly to Grandma. "But we might catch Miss Agatha, at least."

She winked at me. "Both are worth a try."

Miss Agatha wasn't at the edge of the woods anymore. I looked around, but I didn't see her anywhere. Maybe she gave up when she saw there wasn't any food in the trap.

There was nothing to do but hope she'd try again. "Which trap do you want?" I asked.

"I'll take the one in the grass," Cayman said.

I handed him some Seafood Medley in the bowl I'd gotten at the rummage sale. "Put this all the way at the back of the trap, but be careful not to bump the water bottle in the doorway. The trap is really loud when it snaps shut. It might frighten Miss Agatha if she's close by."

"Okay." Cayman walked over to the trap near the woods, and I put my bowl of cat food in the trap near the hydrangea bush.

Then we sat on the ground behind our lawn chairs to wait.

We sat for what seemed like forever. I drew spirals in the dirt with my finger. I listened to birdcalls.

Peter-peter-peter.

Chicka-dee-dee.

I wondered what Cayman was doing. It was hard to see him through the plastic slats of my lawn chair, so I used my fingers to spread two slats open.

Two of his chair slats were spread apart, too. I could just see his eyes.

I tried giving an extra-big smile, so he'd see crinkles around my eyes.

He paused.

I made my eyes bug out.

Then he crossed his eyes.

I bit back a giggle. It was funny to think a silly face could be a peace offering. But I was pretty sure it was.

I moved my mouth up to the space. Then I stuck out my bottom teeth until they touched my top lip, like a dog with a big underbite.

Chicka-dee-dee-dee-dee-dee-dee!

I glanced to see what the chickadee was warning about. Miss Agatha was standing in the grass just beyond the garden.

She looked in the direction of the hydrangea bush. She took a small step.

I rolled the end of the string between my fingers. What if I sneezed and accidentally pulled the string? What if this was my one chance and I blew it?

Miss Agatha took another step. She was definitely headed for my trap.

I glanced through the slats at Cayman. I couldn't see

him very well behind the lawn chair, but his hand came up above the back of the chair.

He gave me a thumbs-up.

Miss Agatha was near my trap now. She walked around it. She smelled the towel that covered the side.

I bit my lip gently as she peeked into the open doorway.

I tightened my hand around the string. *Don't pull it*, I told myself. *Not yet.*

She took a step inside.

Every muscle hurt with wanting to yank the string. But I couldn't pull too soon or too fast. I started counting in my head to give me something to focus on instead of the string. *One, two, three, four, five—*

She took another step inside. Her two front feet were in now. But it was still too early to pull the string.

Six, seven—

Another step. One back foot disappeared inside. *Not yet! Eight—*

Another step. She had almost completely disappeared behind the towel covering the trap. Now only her tail was outside the trap.

So close! Nine—

Her tail flicked and then disappeared inside.

TEN! I pulled the string so hard the water bottle went flying backward and the trap closed with a *snap!*

"Did you get her?" Cayman yelled.

It happened so fast that I wasn't even sure. I tried to get up, but my legs were stiff from sitting still so long that I practically fell over trying to stand. "Can you check?"

Cayman went to the trap and lifted the towel. Miss Agatha was crouched in the very back of the trap.

She hissed.

I grinned with relief. Just like the gyrfalcon, Miss Agatha was fierce enough to fight if she had to. "Everything will be all right," I told her. "Things will be good again, I promise. Even if it doesn't seem like it now."

"What do we do next?" Cayman asked.

"We call Nancy to come get her. Let's push her trap under the hydrangea bush," I said. "At least it's a familiar place for her to wait until Nancy gets here." I didn't want Miss Agatha to be more scared than was necessary. I covered the trap with a towel, and Cayman pushed it under the hydrangea bush.

"Hey, thanks," I said. Now that our job was done, I didn't really know what to say to him. I had so much to tell him, but I didn't want to ruin the tiny bond we'd just made. I knew I'd have to gain some of his trust back before he'd listen to the rest of what I had to say.

"Grandma will be glad we caught her," I said.

Cayman nodded. "I didn't know if it would really work."

"Me either."

At least we made a start, I told myself.

Grandma was waiting for us on the porch.

"Mia caught her!" Cayman said. "Miss Agatha's in her trap under the hydrangea bush."

And I didn't even mind that he told her before I did.

"I guess this might be goodbye, then," Grandma said sadly. "She's a good cat, even if we disagreed about the songbirds."

As I put my arm around her, a car stopped out front.

"Is that Nancy?" I asked, thinking maybe Grandma had called her already.

But Cayman's eyes were wide.

Cayman's mom got out of the car. Her face was red with anger. "I knew you'd be here!" she said. "Didn't I tell you not to come back here anymore?" Then she pointed at Grandma. "And you! Always sticking your nose into things that don't concern you!"

"Mia, please go inside," Grandma said.

I was too shocked to even move.

"Mia, I said go inside," Grandma said in a no-nonsense voice I hardly ever heard from her. *"Now."*

Stepping into the kitchen, I closed the screen door behind me but not the front door. I didn't know what might happen. Grandma might need my help.

Or maybe Cayman might.

Chapter 21

"I never meant to stick my nose in your business or get in the middle between you and Cayman," I heard Grandma say. "You and I are neighbors. I wanted to help."

"I don't need your help," his mom answered sharply.

I wished Grandma hadn't told me to go inside. I wanted to be there with them, not just hear them through the screen door. I especially wanted to see Cayman, because he was silent, stuck in the middle while two people that he loved argued around him.

And I remembered how that felt. When Mom and Dad used to fight, it was like being ripped in half.

"We *all* need help sometimes," Grandma said.

"You might fool Cayman, but I know what you think of me!" Cayman's mom said bitterly.

"I *don't* think you do know what I truly think," Grandma said. "So I will tell you."

I pulled in a sharp breath. The pause was long enough that I worried what Grandma might say. I crept closer to the doorway to peek.

Cayman's mom was red-faced, her eyes narrowed. She looked ready for a fight. I put my hand on the doorknob in case I had to run out to help.

"What I truly think," Grandma said slowly, "is that you've raised a good boy."

Cayman's mom's eyes widened in surprise. Whatever she was expecting Grandma to say, I could tell it wasn't that.

"Cayman never talks about it, but I can see that moving here has been hard," Grandma said. "Starting over and changing always is. There's no shame in accepting help when you can use it."

Cayman's mom turned her head away. "I don't need help," she said, but less firmly than before. Her face looked softer, like the anger was melting away, leaving sadness behind.

"You don't want to feel this way," Grandma said. "Do you?"

Cayman's mom sighed. "There's nothing I can do."

"There's a program," Cayman said. "That birder lady said so, remember? She said she worked for an organization that could help you get better. She left you her card. And I know you still have it because I saw you take it out of the trash after she left."

Anger flashed back into his mother's eyes. "I told you that it's not that easy! I'd have to stay, and who knows how long? I won't leave you. And I won't risk some organization snooping into our business. I've told you what could happen if they do. They might decide to take you away!"

"I'll be fine at home," Cayman said. "I can take care of myself until you get back. Really, I can."

"Or he can stay here," I said through the screen door.

They all turned to look at me.

I had just blurted out what I was thinking. But I meant it.

Stepping out onto the porch, I said, "He can have my room until you're home again. I wouldn't mind at all."

I looked cautiously at Grandma. I hoped she was okay with how I'd just volunteered her house.

She grinned at me. "Yes!" Then she turned to Cayman's

mom. "He's very welcome to stay here until you're home again."

"I won't take charity," she said, crossing her arms over her ribs.

"It's not charity," Grandma said. "It's one neighbor helping another. And my knee is acting up something awful. Cayman can do some things for me while he's here."

I could help Grandma with anything she needed. But she had said sometimes proud people find it easier to give help than take it.

"I don't know," Cayman's mom said slowly. "It would be too much."

Too much of what? Time? Money? Help? I held my breath, afraid that if she left, she'd talk herself out of it.

While she hesitated, a weird angry sound came from the backyard. I was so focused on watching Cayman's mom that for a few seconds I didn't know what it was.

"That's just a stray cat that we've trapped," Grandma said. "Kids, go see if Miss Agatha's all right. Cayman's mom and I will stay here and talk."

"Come on," I said to Cayman. "Maybe Miss Agatha is scared."

I could tell that Cayman didn't want to leave them,

but his mom nodded. "You can call me Sarah," she said to Grandma.

As Cayman and I rounded the corner of Grandma's house, he said, "I don't really want to stay here. But I want her to get better."

"I hope she says yes," I said.

"I don't even know *what* to hope for." Cayman took a deep breath. "I've tried everything I know how to do, but none of it helps enough."

I had "I'm sorry" and "It's not your fault" ready to say, but Grandma said he needed a friend more than pity or advice.

So I just listened.

"She got better for a while, but then she hurt her back," he said. "She had a lot of pain and the medicine didn't help enough. She says drinking is the only thing that makes her feel better." He sighed. "But it doesn't last. It's worse afterward because then she's hurt *and* sad. And it's happening more often since we came here. Moving here was a mistake. Not a good change at all."

"That's because you're still in the middle of it," I said. "That's always the hardest part."

"That birder lady knew as soon as she opened the

door. I could tell by the look on her face. She wrinkled her nose like she smelled alcohol. She said she worked at a place that could help, but Mom slammed the door in her face. She kept her card, though. So I think Mom wants to get help, but I'm the reason she can't. She won't leave me."

"Maybe Grandma will convince her," I said, hoping. "Grandma does get her own way most of the time! She starts talking and, before you know it, you've agreed to something you didn't even see coming."

Cayman gave me a half smile, only one side up. "Yeah, I know what you mean." Then he sighed. "I can't hope very much, though. It's too hard to be disappointed."

"I'll hope extra hard for both of us, then," I said.

He gave me a real smile that time.

Almost at the hydrangea bush, he said, "Would you really be okay if I stayed here?"

"Really," I said.

"If she says yes, I won't be in the way, I promise. I'll give you plenty of time alone with your grandmother."

"Hey, I'm sorry about that," I said, looking down at my feet. "I was jealous at first. But now I'm glad she has a friend to talk birds with when I'm not here. If I've messed up my friendship with you, that's my own fault. But please don't stop being friends with her, too. We both miss you."

"I kind of miss you, too," he said.

I looked up. "Kind of?"

Then I saw the teasing look in his eyes. "Kind of *a lot*," he said.

I smiled. I'd apologized and he'd accepted it. I felt clean and new, like the clearest sunny sky after a thunderstorm.

At the hydrangea bush, Cayman pulled the trap out. "I'll carry the trap with her," he said. "You grab the empty one."

"Okay." But first, I lifted the towel to peek. Miss Agatha was backed into a corner of the trap. She looked smaller than I'd expected.

It'll be okay, I told her in my mind. *You'll probably be coming right back here.*

On the way to the house, Cayman and I both walked as slowly as possible to give Grandma and his mom time to talk.

"Mrs. Wells told me about the big rescue," Cayman said. "It sounded incredible. I'm glad the gyrfalcon was saved."

I nodded. "I wish you'd been there."

Cayman shifted the trap in his hands. "You know

what's strange? I really wanted the gyrfalcon to fly away, but now when I go to the Point, I miss her."

"Grandma calls that happy missing," I said. "It's when you miss something or someone, but you know it's for the best. So you're happy, but you miss them, too."

"Then, yeah," Cayman said. "I guess I do happy miss the gyrfalcon. Did you ever find out what happened to her?"

I shook my head. "Warden Cooper gave me his card and said I could contact him. But I've been afraid to ask. What if she didn't make it? Or what if she lived, but was hurt too badly and now can't ever be free? I'd rather just imagine the best thing happened."

"Maybe it did," Cayman said.

I wanted that to be true. But even so, I couldn't shake the worrying.

As we reached the corner of Grandma's house, Cayman stopped. "Just so you know, I would never take your room. If Mom agrees to go, I have a sleeping bag and I can sleep anywhere."

"Thanks, but if I sleep on the couch, I can sneak into the kitchen and have a midnight snack and no one'll know," I said, grinning.

"Not without me!" That teasing look came back into his eyes. "And as a special thank-you, I'll even let you win and be better than me at some things."

"*Let* me win?" I rolled my eyes. "Yeah, right. Just wait until mini golf. I'll leave you choking on my dust."

"There's no dust in mini golf," he said.

Mr. Right Again. But instead of being annoyed, I said, "I guess you haven't seen me play mini golf, then."

Following him around the corner, I realized it was okay and even fun to be competitive, as long as it didn't become more important than our friendship.

I crossed my fingers hard that everything would work out.

"Come on, Cayman," his mom said. "We're going home."

My hopes crashed. I tried not to let my disappointment show as Cayman handed me the trap with Miss Agatha inside.

"I'll let you know what happens to Miss Agatha," I said. "If you want to know."

He nodded. "Thanks. I'll see you."

Grandma put her arm around me. Her heavy sigh told me she was disappointed, too. I felt like crying, especially when Cayman got into the car and didn't look at us.

"I was hoping Cayman's mom would say yes," I said as they drove away.

"Me too," Grandma said. "But she didn't actually say no. And that means there's room for hope."

I imagined "room for hope" as a real room. In my mind, I made it as big as possible. Not just a regular room but a huge room. A stadium holding as much hope as possible.

But even so, I knew no amount of hope was enough. Cayman's mom had to decide. Just like Warden Cooper had said about the gyrfalcon.

Part of it was up to us, and the rest was up to her.

Chapter 22

That afternoon, I helped Grandma get my room ready. I picked new flowers for the vase on the nightstand, and Grandma put a stack of fresh towels on the bureau.

"Just in case," she said, and we both crossed our fingers.

The sound of a car in the driveway made my heart leap. Running downstairs, I didn't uncross my fingers, hoping that it was Cayman's mom bringing him over.

But it was Nancy picking up Miss Agatha.

"Oh," Grandma said, stepping onto the porch behind me. "Well, that's a good thing, too."

I nodded, even though I couldn't shake that disappointed feeling that it wasn't Cayman. I carried the cage holding Miss Agatha out to Nancy's car.

"You can keep the towel for the shelter," Grandma told

Nancy. Then she lifted up one corner to peek at Miss Agatha. "My cat of mystery," Grandma said, her voice breaking.

I looked over to see tears in Grandma's eyes.

"She'll be in good hands," Nancy promised. "And I'll give you a call after she's settled in and we've had a chance to scan her for a microchip, okay?"

"I'd appreciate that," Grandma said. "She was never really mine, but I've loved her like she was."

"Oh, Grandma," I said, hugging her.

As Nancy got into her car, I called, "Wait!"

I ran into the kitchen and grabbed a bag. I stacked every can of Seafood Medley and Chicken Supreme inside.

"Good idea! It'll help her to have something familiar at the shelter," Nancy said, taking the bag. "Thank you."

Grandma and I stood on the porch until Nancy's car disappeared around the bend.

She squeezed me tight. "I know it's best for her. I'm just sad for me."

"Happy missing?" I asked.

She nodded. "I guess that's one hard part about loving something, isn't it? It hurts when they leave, even if you're happy for them."

Suddenly, I really missed Mom, Dad, Scott, Shelly, and Baby Luke. "And then they get busy with their new life."

Grandma turned to look deeply into my eyes. "Are we still talking about Miss Agatha?" she asked softly. "Or you?"

I shrugged. "Both, I guess. Even with a good change, there are some things to miss."

Grandma nodded. "Always."

I sighed. "Do you suppose only *people* miss things? Or do you think Miss Agatha and the gyrfalcon miss their old homes, too?"

"I think it's possible," Grandma said. "But I also think home can be more than one place."

"A home away from home?" I asked, smiling.

"Exactly," she said.

I sighed. "I guess even a home away from home changes. Coming here was different than I thought it would be. I thought everything would be exactly like I remembered."

"Sometimes it's *you* that changes," Grandma said softly.

I turned to her. *"Me?"*

Grandma nodded. "You're not really my worried little

mouse anymore. Look at you rescuing lost gyrfalcons and stray cats! Who would've believed it?"

I grinned. "And climbing trees!"

Maybe I had changed a bit. Doing those brave things hadn't been so hard, even if they were scary at first. Change is always hard in the middle, but you can't skip that part. You have to go through it to come out the other side.

"Grandma?" I said. "Can I tell you something?"

"Anything," she said.

I took a deep breath. "There are some things that are worrying me about the move," I said. "Bigger things than I've told you before." I felt it all ready to rush out of me, like an untied balloon suddenly let go. "I'm worried Mom and Scott will be disappointed if they find a great house and it's not in my school district. It'll be my fault they couldn't buy it. And I worry that I'll forget things about our old house when Mom, Dad, and I lived there together. And I'm worried that Scott will decide he doesn't like living with a kid."

"Wow!" Grandma said. "That's a lot to worry about. Have you been holding that in all this time?"

I nodded. "Mom is excited to move, and I don't want to ruin that."

"I understand, but I think she'd want to know," Grandma said. "Do you want to know what I think?"

"Yes," I said.

"I think if you have to change schools, you will face it. You've always made friends wherever you've gone to school before."

"But I don't want to," I said.

"No, but you could if you had to," Grandma said. "Am I right?"

I nodded. "I guess."

"Then that worry has no true power over you," she said. "You have slayed it by knowing it wouldn't break you if it happened. I'm not saying it would be easy. I'm not saying it's what you want. But you could face it if you had to."

"Okay," I said. "Maybe so."

"Now, about the memories you're afraid of losing. Why don't you write them down? That's a way to hold on to them."

I thought about it. "I could imagine walking through our house and write down everything that comes to mind."

"Perfect!" Grandma said. "And about Scott, can I tell you a secret?"

"Of course," I said.

"I couldn't stand him when I first met him!"

My jaw dropped. "No! Really?"

"I thought he was a boring wet blanket! Like the red-and-white-petunia-and-geranium crowd at the Stone Harbor Garden Club. No sparkle or imagination or sense of fun! And I told Beanie that."

"Wow. What did she say?"

"She was hurt," Grandma said. "And I realized something really important. It didn't really matter what I thought of Scott. He makes her happy and, more than anything else, I want her to be happy. It wasn't fair of me to put her in the middle and make her choose between us. So I tried seeing him through Beanie's eyes, and you know what? It worked! Scott and I don't enjoy the same things, but we both love her. And that's enough to start with. But then, before I knew it, I liked him, too."

"I'm glad," I said.

"Maybe Scott didn't have plans for kids before he met you. But plans and people can change, Mia. He loves Beanie and he loves you. I can see it in the way he looks at you both. It'll be an adjustment, but he won't change his mind." She laughed. "And if he ever did, you'll come live with me!"

It felt like a huge heavy weight had been lifted off me. Grandma was right. Once you faced a worry, it didn't have as much power over you.

As I laughed with her, a car stopped out front.

Cayman got out of the car with his sleeping bag and a suitcase. I felt hope rush into me, filling me all the way from my head to my feet. Could it be? Had his mother changed her mind?

He waved to his mother. Then he turned toward us. "She's going to try it."

I grinned, but he looked so alone standing there in the driveway with his sleeping bag. I rushed down to grab his suitcase to carry it for him.

"Welcome to your home away from home," I said.

Chapter 23

That night as we were eating supper, Nancy called. Grandma put the call on speaker, so we could all hear.

When they'd scanned Miss Agatha, they'd found a microchip.

"When we called the number, the woman was so happy that she started crying," Nancy said. "She was here on vacation back in March, and Miss Agatha—well, Harriet—slipped out the door while someone was bringing in groceries. They were heartbroken when they couldn't find her! They finally had to return home to New Hampshire. They'd given up hope of ever seeing her again. But when they walked into the room, Harriet knew them immediately! She started purring as soon as they picked her up."

"Thank you, Nancy. We're glad for Miss—Harriet," Grandma said. "Thank you for letting us know. She's back where she belongs."

After she hung up, a sudden silence hit us all. The excitement of knowing Miss Agatha had a family was replaced by a hard understanding. She was gone for good.

"To be honest, part of me hoped they wouldn't find a microchip," Grandma finally said. "I had a silly idea that I'd adopt her myself."

"Not a silly idea," I said. Also not a surprise.

"I thought she'd be yours, too," Cayman said. "I wish she had been."

"I can't help feeling sad, but it's better to know the truth," Grandma said. "Otherwise you always wonder."

Was it always better to know the truth? What if the news was bad? Even so, I knew Grandma was right. Wondering ate away at you. It kept you stuck, spinning like a leaf in a whirlpool, unable to move on.

And not knowing didn't change the truth.

Right then I knew I didn't want to be stuck wondering anymore. There were two things I needed to know. I needed to ask Mom about moving and I needed to ask

Warden Cooper what happened to the gyrfalcon.

Just deciding to ask made me feel relieved, and I didn't even know the answers yet. But whatever Mom and Warden Cooper said, I felt brave enough to hear it.

"Okay, kids." Grandma picked up her dishes to carry them to the sink. "No more sad thoughts. What shall we do tonight? Let's do something fun."

I could tell Grandma was trying to change the mood. I wanted something comforting and familiar that would let us be a little silly. "Candy Land?" I asked.

"Candy Land?" Cayman said. "Are you kidding me?"

"Have you ever played it?" I asked.

"Of course." He rolled his eyes. "When I was *five*."

"Good. I don't have to explain the rules, then," I said. "I call the yellow gingerbread man as my token!"

"Green is my favorite color," Grandma said.

"Red or blue?" I asked Cayman. "And get ready to eat yellow gingerbread dust."

He sighed, but I saw a little smile, even though he was trying to hide it. "Blue."

That night, I texted Mom and asked how the house hunt was going. **I love you and I miss you. Please tell**

Scott that I love and miss him, too, I ended. Then I texted Warden Cooper and asked what happened to the gyrfalcon.

Now I could deal with the truth—whatever it was.

Mom called me. "I love and miss you, too! Scott says the house is too quiet without you," she said. "He's been packing your books carefully. Our house has an offer already."

So that was it. We were definitely moving.

I took a deep breath. "Wow," I said. "That was fast."

"Yes, and I think we've found a great new house," Mom said. "I can't wait for you to see it! It has a wonderful bedroom for you overlooking some woods. We can even match your old blue paint if you want. I saved a paint chip."

I opened my mouth to say yes about the blue paint. But then I stopped. I'd picked that color years ago. Did I really still want it? Or was it like vanilla ice cream— familiar and comfortable, but better for an "old me," not who I was now?

For the first time, I didn't feel scared about moving. I knew I'd get through it. As long as I had Mom and Scott, we'd make it work.

Because home isn't just a place, it's the people you're with.

"No, I think I want a new color," I said. "I'm ready for a change."

Chapter 24

A few days later, Grandma drove Cayman and me an hour away up the coast. Warden Cooper had replied mysteriously to my text asking about the gyrfalcon.

Are you busy next Tuesday at 11 a.m.? I'll send you the address.

On the ride, I thought we were going to the bird hospital. But the address took us to a boat launch at a small cove on the ocean. In the parking lot, I saw Warden Cooper sitting at a picnic table with a big dog carrier by his side.

Cayman and I were out of the car in a flash.

The gyrfalcon looked at me through the carrier door. A shiver went between my shoulders. That fierce fire had returned to her dark, yellow-rimmed eyes. She was still the most beautiful bird I'd ever seen.

I'll always remember you, I told her in my mind.

"At first it was touch and go at the bird hospital," Warden Cooper said. "But once they'd fixed her up and she'd had plenty to eat, her strength came back. She aced every flight test. Then she made it clear that she was anxious to be on her way. I knew you'd want to say goodbye."

"Yes! Thank you," I said.

"But why are you letting her go here?" Cayman asked.

"I wanted a quiet spot. I didn't want to risk having an audience," Warden Cooper said. "She might stick around here awhile. She'll have her best chance if we don't attract too much attention."

I nodded. "I won't even take photos. I'll keep my phone in my pocket." When I'd first arrived, I would've itched to take a photo, but today that wasn't as important as keeping the gyrfalcon safe. And I didn't want to see the moment on a screen. I wanted to just experience it myself, with nothing between her and me.

"Then let's set this little girl free," Warden Cooper said. "It's a perfect day for flying. A blue sky with a breeze to help her on her way."

My hands were tingling with excitement as he brought

the carrier down to the beach, but I also felt a little empty knowing this was goodbye.

"She's a powerful bird, and we don't know which direction she'll go," Warden Cooper said, unlocking the fasteners around the edges of the carrier. "You don't want to be in her way. So, everyone, please take three steps backward."

Grandma, Cayman, and I did. One. Two. Three.

"When I lift off the top of the carrier, don't blink!" Warden Cooper said. "Sometimes this all happens really fast!"

I didn't know if he was kidding or not, but I stared without blinking just in case.

As soon as he removed the top of the carrier, the gyrfalcon lifted her head. For a few seconds she stayed still. Maybe she didn't realize she was free.

Then her wings unfolded, big and wide and snowy white, speckled with black. She pumped them once and hopped out of the carrier and onto the beach.

She was still magnificent. Fierce and magical, like a bird from a fantasy book. As she looked around her, I held my breath. It was thrilling to be so close to her when she was free.

You can do this. Just figure it out as you go, I told her in my mind. *The Arctic is waiting for you to come home.*

Then, with another wing flap, she leaped into the air!

"There she goes!" I cried as she rose upward out over the water. She pumped her wings and flew. High above us, she circled and then let out a wild, spine-shivery scream, like freedom and wildness just exploded out of her.

"I think she was saying goodbye," Cayman said.

We stood there watching her head up the coast away from us, until she was just a fleck in the sky. I was so full of happy missing that I couldn't even speak. I didn't have one photo to remember that moment and yet I knew I'd never forget it.

And then even the fleck was gone.

"She's headed back," Warden Cooper said.

"To the Point?" I asked, concerned.

Warden Cooper shook his head. "Back home. She flew due north."

I imagined the gyrfalcon flying past islands and trees and over miles and miles of ocean until icebergs appeared below her. Back where she belonged, where she could let loose that wild call and someone would answer her, "Welcome home."

In a few weeks, when Mom came to get me, I knew I'd be ready to go home, too. Even though home would be a new house and some things would be different or hard, I'd be okay.

The gyrfalcon and I had flown in together, and we'd changed each other. I didn't need her to have fierce courage for both of us anymore.

I had some of my own.

As we got into the car to go home, Grandma said, "We have a long to-do list today! The mini golf place is practically on the way home. And then I want to stop at the Humane Society."

Cayman and I looked at each other, surprised.

"I thought Miss Agatha's family came and got her?" Cayman asked.

"They did indeed," Grandma said.

"So why do you need to go to the Humane Society?" I asked.

"Well, I've never had a cat before, and I can't truly say that I 'had' Miss Agatha," Grandma said. "But now I don't think I can live without one."

"You're getting a cat?" I asked, excited.

"Maybe two," Grandma said.

"Two!" I burst out laughing.

"Nancy says there is a lovely bonded pair of cats up for adoption at the Humane Society. Their owner died, and they've been together for their whole lives. They've only ever lived indoors, so we won't have to disagree about the songbirds. I thought we'd go have a look."

I grinned. No way we were just *looking*. Knowing Grandma, those cats were definitely coming home with us.

"You can help me make them feel comfortable," Grandma said. "And I suppose we'll need a few things. Assuming we bring them home, of course."

Cayman smiled at me. "I'm assuming we *are* bringing them home."

"Me too," I said. "When we get back, Cayman and I can walk to Holbrook's and get some cat food. Since I gave all Miss Agatha's away."

"Yes, and why don't you get some ice cream, too?" Grandma said. "I was surprised to see we're out."

I blushed. Cayman and I had finished the carton of ice cream the night before. It had become our nightly routine to meet in the kitchen for a midnight snack. "Do you think we could get chocolate chip this time?" I asked.

"Absolutely!" Grandma said.

I looked over at Cayman and smiled. "We're getting a pet!" I whispered to him.

"Two!" he whispered back.

This trip hadn't been what I expected—and it kept surprising me. But even though change is scary, it brings new things, too. New friends. New adventures. New challenges. New chances.

And sometimes, even a new you.

And about *that*—I wouldn't change a thing.

About the Author

Cynthia Lord is the award-winning author of *Rules*, a Newbery Honor book and a Schneider Family Book Award winner, as well as the critically acclaimed *Because of the Rabbit*, *A Handful of Stars*, *Half a Chance*, and *Touch Blue*. She is also the author of the Shelter Pet Squad chapter book series and the Hot Rod Hamster picture books and readers. Lord is a former teacher, behavioral specialist, and bookseller. She lives in Maine with her family, a dog, and three pet rabbits. She and her family have also fostered over twenty-five rescue bunnies. Visit her at cynthialord.com.